"I like it here, Buck," Gina said.

"I think God may have sent me and Bobby here for a reason. I'm thinking maybe I'd like to stay."

His ambivalence must have shown on his face, because she cocked her head to one side and spoke. "That bothers you, doesn't it? How come? Is it about my resemblance to your late wife?"

"Somewhat." Actually, he was starting to wonder how he'd ever mistaken her for Ivana. She had a plucky strength and determination, a set to her chin and a way of holding herself that were all completely her own. Still, he had questions.

"Look," she said, "I'm sorry if I bring up memories for you. Maybe I'll get on my feet quickly and be able to get out of here. But meanwhile…"

"Meanwhile, what?" He was holding her baby in the rainy twilight, looking at her and finding her beautiful, and feeling like he might be stepping into the biggest mess of his life.

Lee Tobin McClain read *Gone with the Wind* in the third grade and has been a hopeless romantic ever since. When she's not writing angst-filled love stories with happy endings, she's getting inspiration from her church singles group, her gymnastics-obsessed teenage daughter, and her rescue dog and cat. In her day job, Lee gets to encourage aspiring romance writers in Seton Hill University's low-residency MFA program. Visit her at leetobinmcclain.com.

Books by Lee Tobin McClain

Love Inspired

Rescue River

Engaged to the Single Mom
His Secret Child
Small-Town Nanny
The Soldier and the Single Mom

Lone Star Cowboy League: Boys Ranch

The Nanny's Texas Christmas

The Soldier and the Single Mom

Lee Tobin McClain

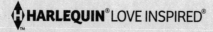

Recycling programs
for this product may
not exist in your area.

LOVE INSPIRED BOOKS

ISBN-13: 978-0-373-21413-6

The Soldier and the Single Mom

www.Harlequin.com

Printed in U.S.A.

Therefore if any man be in Christ,
he is a new creature: old things are
passed away; behold, all things are become new.

—*2 Corinthians* 5:17

To Porter, the real-world model for Spike.
Rescue pets rule!

Chapter One

It was 2:00 a.m. on a mild March night when Buck Armstrong saw his dead wife walking toward the town of Rescue River, Ohio, carrying their baby on one hip.

He swerved, hit the brakes and skidded onto the gravel berm. On the seat beside him, Crater—his chosen companion for the night—let out a yip.

Buck passed his hand over his eyes. It wasn't real—couldn't be. He'd made similar mistakes before, when he was tired, when the war memories came back too strong. Tonight, driving home from assisting in an emergency surgery out at the dog rescue, he wanted nothing more than to keep driving past the turnoff to the liquor store, lock himself in his room and shut it all off until morning.

He looked again, squinting through the moonlit fog.

They were still there. But they were running away from him, or rather, his wife was. Baby Mia was gone.

Where was the baby? He scrambled out of the truck, leaving the door ajar. "Stay!" he ordered the dog automatically as he took off toward his wife. "Ivana! Wait!"

She ran faster, but Buck had gotten back into military shape since he'd quit drinking, and he caught up easily. Was relieved to see that the baby was now in front of her, in some sort of sling.

His hand brushed against her soft hair.

She screamed, spun away from him, and he saw her face.

It wasn't his wife, but someone else. A complete stranger.

He stopped, his heart pounding triple time. Sweat formed on his forehead as he tried to catch his breath. "I'm sorry. I thought you were—"

"Leave us alone," she ordered, stepping away, one arm cradled protectively at the back of the baby's head, the other going to her oversize bag. "I have a gun."

"Whoa." He took a couple of steps back, hands lifting to shoulder height, palms out. A giant stone of disappointment pressed down on him. "I don't mean you any harm. I thought you were… Never mind."

A breeze rattled the leaves of a tall oak tree beside the road. He caught the rich scent of newly turned earth, plowed dirt, fields ready for planting. Up ahead, a spotlight illuminated the town's well-known sign, kept up and repainted yearly since Civil War days: Rescue River, Ohio. All Are Welcome, All Are Safe.

Ivana had been so proud of their hometown's history as a station on the Underground Railroad, its reputation for embracing outsiders of all types, races and creeds.

The good people of Rescue River had even put up with the damaged man he'd been when he'd returned from war, until he'd repeatedly broken their trust.

"Go back to your truck," the woman ordered, hand still in her bag. Now that he could see her better, he realized she was sturdier than Ivana had been, with square shoulders and a determined set to her chin. Same long tawny hair, but fuller lips and big gray-blue eyes that were now glaring at him. "Do it. Back in the truck, now."

He should do what she said, should turn around right now and get on home before the memories that were chasing him caught up.

Should, but when had he ever done what he should? "What are you doing out here in the middle of the night, ma'am? Can I give you a ride somewhere?"

She laughed without humor, shaking her

head. "No way, buddy. Just drive away. We'll all be better off."

He had to admire her courage if not her common sense. There was no good reason for a woman with a baby to be wandering the countryside, but she was acting as if she owned the whole state.

"Sure you don't want me to call someone?" Truth was, he felt relieved. He could go home and crash and try to forget that, just for a minute, he'd gotten the crazy hope that Ivana and the baby were still alive, that he'd get a second chance to love them the way they deserved.

"We're fine." She ran a hand through her hair and patted the baby who, somehow, still slept against her chest. He caught sight of wispy hair, heard that sweet, nestling-in sigh of a contented little one.

Pain stabbed his heart.

She did seem fine, perfectly able to defend herself, he argued against the faint whisper of chivalry that said he shouldn't let a woman and child stay out here in the middle of the night. After all, he wasn't much of a protector. He'd lost as many people as he'd saved in Afghanistan. And as for Ivana and Mia…

The sound of a mournful howl silenced his thoughts. Crater. "It's okay, buddy," he called, and the scarred rottweiler bounded out of the truck's cab. As Crater jumped up on him, Buck rubbed the dog's sides and let him lick his face and, for the first time since seeing the woman, he felt his heart rate settle.

"Let's go home," he said to the dog. But Crater had different ideas, and he lunged playfully toward the woman and baby. Buck snapped his fingers and the dog sank into a sitting position, looking back toward him. The deep scar on the dog's back, for which they'd named him out at the rescue, shone pale in the moonlight.

"That's a well-trained dog." The woman cocked her head to one side.

"He's a sweetheart. Come on, boy."

The dog trotted to his side, and as they

started back to his truck, Buck felt his heart rate calm a little more. Yeah, his shrink was right: he was a prime candidate for a service dog. Except he couldn't make the commitment. As soon as he'd paid off his debts and made amends where he could, he was out of here, and who knew whether he'd end up in a dog-friendly place?

"Hey, hold on a minute." The woman's voice was the slightest bit husky.

He turned but didn't walk back toward her. Didn't look at her. It hurt too much. She was still a reminder of Ivana and all he'd lost. "What?"

"Maybe you *could* give us a hand. Or a ride."

Buck drew in a deep breath and blew it out. "Okay, sure," he said, trying not to show his reluctance to be in her company a moment longer. After all, he'd made the offer, so courtesy dictated he should follow through. "Where are you headed?"

"That's a good question," she said, lifting the baby a little to take the weight off her chest.

He remembered Ivana doing that very same thing with Mia. He swallowed.

"What kind of a town is Rescue River?"

"It's a real nice town." It was, too. He'd consider staying on there himself if he hadn't burned so many bridges.

"Think I could find a cheap room? Like, really cheap?"

He cocked his head to one side. "The only motel had no vacancy, last I saw. My sister's renovating what's going to be a guesthouse, but it's not open for another few months…"

"Does she have a room that's done, or mostly done? We don't need much."

Buck wanted to lie, would have lied, except he seemed to hear Ivana's voice in his head. Quoting Scripture, trying to coax him along the path to believing. Something about helping widows and orphans in their distress.

This woman might or might not be a widow, but to be out walking the rural Ohio roads in the wee hours surely indicated some kind of distress.

"She's got a couple of rooms close to done," he admitted.

"Do you think she'd let me rent one?"

He frowned. "I don't know. Lacey's not the most trusting person in the world. A late-night guest she isn't expecting won't sit well with her."

The comment hung between them for an awkward moment. It was the simple truth, though. Or maybe not so simple. The fact that the pretty stranger had a baby would disturb Lacey. A lot.

The woman gave him a skeptical look, then straightened and turned away. "Okay. Thanks."

Squeezing his eyes shut for just a second, he turned and tried to head back toward his truck. She wasn't his responsibility. He had enough on his plate just to keep himself together.

Nope. Like a fool, he turned around. "Hey,

wait. Come on. We'll try to talk Lacey into letting you stay. At least for the night."

"That would be wonderful," she said, a relieved smile breaking out on her face.

Wonderful for her, maybe. Not for him. The last thing he needed was an Ivana look-alike, with a baby no less, staying one thin wall away from him.

"My name's Gina, by the way." She shifted the diaper bag and held out a hand.

"Buck Armstrong." He reached out, wrapped his oversize hand around her soft, delicate fingers and wished he'd driven home another way.

Gina Patterson climbed into the backseat of the handsome stranger's extended-cab pickup, her heart thudding. *Please, Lord, keep us safe. Watch over us.*

Don't let him be a serial killer.

But a dog wouldn't be that friendly with a serial killer, and a serial killer wouldn't act that loving with a dog. Would they?

"Air bags," she explained when he looked over his shoulder, eyebrows raised. "Can't sit in front." Technically, she shouldn't even bring Bobby into the truck, not without a car seat, only she couldn't figure out what else to do. She couldn't give Buck the keys to get her car seat from her out-of-gas SUV, and she certainly couldn't leave Bobby with him while she walked the three miles back to her vehicle.

They were safer in the backseat, she figured, safe from him as well as from any kind of car accident. If he tried to kidnap them, she could at least hit him in the back of the head with her shoe.

She was ready to drop with fatigue after three long days of driving, and it was getting colder by the minute. Buck's arrival had to be the blessing she'd prayed for. Although he seemed pretty gruff for a rescuer.

"Right, I knew that. It's less than a mile," he said, and his dog panted back over the seat at her, smiling in the way happy dogs did.

It made her miss her poodles, but she knew her best friend back home would take care of them.

She scratched the dog's ears for a minute and then let her head sag back against the seat, thanking God again for keeping her and Bobby safe during their journey.

Well, mostly safe. She'd been foolish to leave her bag on the sink while she'd changed Bobby's diaper. Who'd have thought there'd be a purse thief in a rest area in rural Indiana? Fortunately, she'd filled her tank just before the theft—with cash—so she'd kept going as far as she could, leaving the interstate so there'd be less of a trail.

The debit card she'd kept in her jacket pocket might help in the future, once things back home cooled down, but she didn't dare use it now.

After the theft, she'd gotten scared and timed things all wrong. She'd thought she could make it to a hotel she'd seen advertised in a larger town up ahead, but the SUV was a gas hog and had sputtered to a stop a few miles back.

At which point she'd realized she didn't have enough cash for a hotel, anyway.

"All set?" Buck looked back at her and Bobby, brows raised over eyes the color of the ocean on a cloudy day.

Man, those were some haunted eyes. "We're set. Thank you for helping us."

She studied the back of him as he put the truck into gear and drove into the town. Broad shoulders, longish hair and stubble that made him look like a bad boy.

What had *he* been doing out at 2:00 a.m.? The question only now occurred to her, now that she and Bobby were safe, or seemed to be. "Excuse me," she said, leaning forward, "but you haven't been drinking or...partying, have you?"

His shoulders stiffened. "No. Why?"

Whew. She hadn't smelled alcohol on him, but alcohol wasn't the only thing that could mess you up. Her husband had been an old hand at covering his addiction to cocaine, right up until he'd lost control on a California mountain and skied headlong into a tree. The drugs had shown up in the autopsy blood work, but when he'd left the ski chalet an hour earlier, she hadn't even known he was impaired. Yet another mistake her in-laws had laid at her feet.

Her throat tightened and she crammed the memories back down. "Just wondering."

So maybe she'd done the right thing after all. When Bobby had started to cry, she'd decided it was better to risk walking than to stay with her vehicle. She'd scraped together change from the floor and found her emergency twenty in the bin between the driver's and passenger's seats. So at least she could get Bobby some food. At ten months, he needed way more than mother's milk.

Hopefully, she could find a church that would take her in, because calling in her lost wallet might put the police on her trail. She chewed on her lower lip.

How had she ever gotten into this situation? She tried to tell herself it wasn't her fault. While she'd committed to stay with her husband, she hadn't married her in-laws. Once he was gone, so was her obligation to them. When Bobby was old enough to know the whole story, he could choose to reconnect in a safe way if he wanted to.

"Guesthouse is right up there." Buck waved a hand, causing Gina to look around and realize that Rescue River was a cute little town, the kind with sidewalks and shops and glowing streetlamps, a moonlit church on one corner and a library on the other. The kind of safe haven where she might be able to breathe for a little while and figure out her options.

Except that, without ID and with just a twenty and change, her options seemed very limited. Worry cramped her belly.

The stranger pulled up in front of a rambling brick home. The outdoor light was on, revealing a porch swing and a front-door wreath made of flowers and pretty branches.

"I'll have to wake up my sister. You can wait here in the truck or out front." He gestured toward the house.

Well, okay, then. No excess of manners.

Except that, actually, she was the stranger and he was doing her a service. "I'll wait on the porch. Thanks."

He seemed able to read her mind as he came around to open the truck door for her. "Sorry to leave you outside, but my sister is sort of touchy," he said as they walked up the narrow brick walkway. "I can't bring a stranger in to set up shop without asking permission. It's her place." He paused. "It's a very safe town, but I'll leave Crater out here if that will make you more comfortable."

"It will, thanks." It had been the dog, and the stranger's reaction to the dog, that had made her decide he was a reliable person to help her.

That, and the fact that she was desperate.

In her worst moments she wondered if she'd done the right thing, taking Bobby away from her in-laws' wealth and security. But no way. They'd become more and more possessive of him, trying to push her out of the picture and care for him themselves. And she kept coming back to what she'd seen: her mother-in-law holding Bobby out for her father-in-law to hit, hard, causing the baby to wail in pain. Her father-in-law *had* started to shake Bobby, she was sure of it, despite their vigorous denials and efforts to turn the criticism back on her.

Once she knew for sure, she couldn't in good conscience stay herself, or leave Bobby in his grandparents' care.

When she'd first driven away from the mansion that had felt increasingly like a prison, relief had made her giddy. She'd not known how oppressed she had felt, living there, until she'd started driving across the country with no forwarding address. Realizations about her dead husband's problems had stacked up, one on top of the other, until she was overwhelmed with gratitude to God for helping her escape the same awful consequences for herself and Bobby.

As she'd crossed state lines, though, doubts had set in, so that now her dominant, gnawing emotion was fear. How would she make a living? What job could she get without references and with few marketable skills? And while she worked, who would watch Bobby? She wouldn't leave her precious baby with just anyone. She had to be able to trust them. To know they'd love and care for him in her absence.

Inside the house, a door slammed. "I've about had it, Buck!"

She heard Buck's voice, lower, soothing, though she couldn't make out the words.

"You've got to be kidding. She has a baby with her?"

More quiet male talk.

The door to the guesthouse burst open, and a woman about her age, in a dark silk robe, stood, hands on hips. "Okay, spill it. What's your story?"

The woman's tone raised Gina's hackles, whooshing her back to her in-laws and their demanding glares. The instinct to walk away was strong, but she had Bobby to consider. She drew in a breath and let it out slowly, a calming technique from her yoga days. "Long version or short?"

"I work all day and then come home and try to renovate this place. I'm tired."

"Short, then. My purse was stolen, I'm out of gas and I need a place to stay."

The woman frowned. "For how long?"

"I…don't know. A couple of days."

"Why can't you call someone?"

That was the key question. How did she explain how she'd gotten so isolated from her childhood friends, how she'd needed to go to a part of the country where she didn't know anyone, both to make a fresh start and so that her in-laws didn't find her? "That's in the long version."

"So…" The woman cocked her head to one side, studying her with skepticism in every angle of her too-thin frame. "Are you part of some scam?"

"Lacey." Buck put a hand on the woman's shoulder. "If you're opening a guesthouse, you need to be able to welcome people."

"If you're serious about recovery from your drinking problem, you need to stop pulling stunts like this."

Buck winced.

Gina reached up to rub her aching shoulder. Great. Another addict.

The woman drew in a breath, visibly trying to remain calm. "I'm sorry. But you're blinded by how she looks like Ivana. Stuff like this happens all the time in big cities. We have to be careful."

Bobby stirred and let out a little cry, and as Gina swayed to calm him, something inside her hardened. She was tired of explaining herself to other people. If she weren't in such dire straits, she'd walk right down those pretty, welcoming porch steps and off into the night. "You can search me. All I've got is this diaper bag." She shifted and held it out to the woman. "It's hard to run a scam with an infant tagging along."

Buck raised his eyebrows but didn't comment, and scarily enough, she could read what he was thinking. *So you don't have a gun in there.*

Of course she didn't.

The woman, Lacey, took it, set it down on the table and pawed through.

Gina's stomach tightened.

Bobby started to cry in earnest. "Shh," she soothed. He needed a diaper change, a feeding and bed. She could only hope the trauma and changes of the past few days wouldn't damage him, that her own love and commitment and consistency would be enough.

"Look, you can stay tonight and we'll talk in the morning." With a noisy sigh, the woman turned away, but not before Gina saw a pained expression on her face. "*You* settle her in," she said to Buck. "Put her in the Escher." She stormed inside, letting the screen door bang behind her.

Buck felt tired, inescapably tired, but also keyed up to where he knew he wasn't going to sleep. "Come on," he said to the beautiful stranger.

But she didn't follow. "This isn't going to work out. I'll find something else."

"There's no place else." He picked up her bag and beckoned her inside, with Crater padding behind him. "Don't worry, Lacey will be more hospitable in the morning." Maybe. He knew what else had bothered Lacey, besides the fact that she'd rescued him one too many times from some late-night escapade: Gina's little boy. Just last year, Lacey had miscarried the baby who was all she had left of her soldier husband. Seeing someone who apparently wasn't taking good care of her own child had to infuriate her.

He wasn't sure his sister's judgment was fair; Gina might be doing the best she could for her baby, might be on the run from some danger worse than whatever she'd be likely to face on an Ohio country road.

He led her through the vinyl sheeting and raw boards that were the future breakfast room, up the stairs and into the hallway that housed the guest rooms. "Here's the only other finished one, besides mine," he said, stopping at the room called the Escher. He opened the door and let her enter before him, ordering Crater to lie down just inside the door.

Gina looked around, laughing with apparent delight. "This is amazing!"

The bed appeared to float and the walls held prints by a modern artist Buck had only recently learned about. The nightstand was made to look like it was on its side, and the rug created an optical illusion of a spiraling series of stair steps.

"Lacey was an art history major in college," he explained. "She's hoping to coordinate with the new art museum to attract guests."

"That's so cool!" Gina walked from picture to picture, joggling the baby so he wouldn't fuss. "I love Escher."

He felt a reluctant flash of liking for this woman who could spare the energy for art appreciation at a time like this. He also noticed that she knew who Escher was, which was more than he had, until Lacey had educated him.

His curiosity about Gina kicked up a notch. She appeared to be destitute and basically homeless, but she was obviously educated. He scanned her slim-fitting trousers and crisp shirt: definitely expensive. Those diamond studs in her ears looked real.

So why'd she been walking along a country road at night?

She put the baby down on the bed and pulled out a diaper pad. "Sorry, he needs a change."

"Sheets and towels here," he said, tapping a cabinet. "There might even be soap. Gina already let one couple stay here for a honeymoon visit."

She turned to him, one hand on the baby's chest. "I can't tell you how grateful I am."

"No problem." Though it was. "I'll be right next door if you need anything."

She swallowed visibly. "Okay."

Unwanted compassion hit him. She was alone and scared in a strange place. "Look, Lacey is a real light sleeper. She'll wake up if there's any disturbance. And... I can leave Crater here if you want a guard dog."

"Thank you. That would be wonderful." She put a hand on his arm. "You've been amazing."

He didn't need her touching him. He backed away so quickly he bumped against the open door. "Stay, boy," he ordered Crater and then let himself out.

And stood in the hallway, listening to her cooing to her baby while a battle waged inside him. He wanted a drink in the worst way.

He reached down, but of course, Crater

wasn't there to calm him. He took one step toward the front door. Stopped. Tried to picture his recovery mentor.

Wondered whether the bar out by the highway was still open.

Ten minutes later, after a phone call to his mentor, he tossed restlessly in his bed. It was going to be a long night.

Chapter Two

A hoarse shout woke Gina out of a restless sleep.

Instinctively, she reached for Bobby. She found him in the nest she'd made with rolled blankets and towels. Thankfully, he slept on through more shouted words she couldn't distinguish in her sleepy state.

Sweat broke out on her body as she lay completely still, just as she'd done so many nights when her husband had come home drunk or high. Hoping, praying he'd sleep downstairs rather than coming up in the mood for some kind of interaction, whether affection or a fight. None of it ever ended well when he'd been using. Sometimes, his rage took physical form.

A knock on the door made her heart pound harder, but then she realized it came from the next room. She heard the clink of an old-fashioned key in a lock. A woman's murmuring voice: "It's okay, Buck. It's okay. You had another nightmare."

It all came clear to her: the guesthouse. The unfriendly landlady. Buck's haunted eyes.

Sounded like he'd had a nightmare and his sister had come to wake him out of it.

She drew in a breath and rubbed Bobby's back, comforted by the steady sound of his breathing. She'd landed in a safe place for the moment. The edges of the sky were just starting to brighten through the window, but she didn't have to deal with her day just yet. She could sleep again.

There were more murmurs next door. A hall door opened and closed. A toilet flushed. Then silence again.

Surprisingly enough, she did drop back to sleep.

* * *

"Good morning!" Gina walked into the kitchen the next morning with Bobby on her hip. He'd woken up hungry, and she'd nursed him and fed him her last jar of baby food. It was time to figure out her next step.

"Hey." Lacey's voice sounded unenthusiastic. She wore scrubs and sat with a cup of coffee in front of her. Her eyes were puffy and underlined by dark shadows.

No wonder, given last night's drama.

Lacey obviously wasn't going to make conversation, so Gina soldiered on. "Thank you so much for giving me and Bobby a place to sleep last night."

"Sure." Lacey glanced up from her newspaper and then went back to reading an article on the local news page.

"You headed to work?" Gina asked. "What do you do?"

The woman tried to smile, but it was obviously an effort. "I'm a CNA. Certified Nursing Assistant. And yeah, I leave in half an hour." A large orange cat wove its way between her legs and then jumped into her lap, and she ran her hands over it as if for comfort.

"You want me to fix you breakfast?"

That made Lacey look up. "What?"

"I'm a pretty good cook. If you're going to work, you need more than coffee."

Lacey let out a reluctant chuckle. "Is that so, Mom?"

Buck walked into the room, stretching and yawning hugely. He wore a plain, snug-fitting white T-shirt and faded jeans.

Gina swallowed hard. Okay. Yeah. He was handsome. At least, if you didn't look into the abyss that seemed to live permanently behind his eyes.

"How's everyone this morning?" he asked in a forced, cheerful tone.

Lacey pointed at Gina with her coffee cup. "She offered to cook breakfast."

"Sounds good to me," Buck said. "I've got comp time at the clinic from last night, so I'm gonna work on the house today. Could use some fuel, for sure."

Lacey waved a hand toward the refrigerator and stove. "Knock yourself out," she said to Gina.

Gina shifted Bobby and walked over to Lacey. "Any chance you could hold him? His name's Bobby, by the way."

Lacey scooted away so fast that the chair leg scraped along the freshly polished wood floor, leaving a raw scratch. "No, thanks. I... My hands are full with Mr. Whiskers."

Buck was there in a fraction of a second, concern all over his face. "I'll take him."

Gina cocked her head at the two of them, curious. She'd never met a woman who wasn't charmed by her son, especially when he was newly fed and changed, cooing and smiling.

Buck, on the other hand, held Bobby like a pro, bouncing him on his knee and tickling his tummy to make him laugh.

Gina rummaged in the refrigerator and found eggs, some Havarti cheese and green onions. It was enough to make a good-tasting scramble. Thick slices of bread went alongside, and she found some apples to cut up as a garnish.

When she placed the plates in front of the two of them a few minutes later, they both looked surprised, and when Lacey tasted the eggs, she actually smiled. "Not bad."

"I like to cook." Gina cleared her throat. "Is there any work you need done today? I have to find a way to get some gas out to my car, but other than that, I'd love to spend a few hours working around here in exchange for your letting me stay last night."

Lacey waved a hand. "Don't worry about it. This breakfast is payment enough."

"Truth is," Gina said, her face heating, "I might need to impose on you for another night. So we could consider it advance payment."

The other woman studied her thoughtfully. "Can you handle an honest answer?"

"Of course."

"I have a hard time trusting someone who

can't afford a hotel but can afford shoes like that." She gestured at Gina's designer loafers.

Gina looked down at the soft leather and felt a moment's shallow regret. She wouldn't be wearing shoes like this anymore, that was for sure.

"She could work this morning while I'm here," Buck interjected. "We need cleanup help, and anyone could do that. And this afternoon, she can work on getting her car and whatever else she needs to do."

Gina gripped the edge of her chair for courage. Asking for favors wasn't her favorite thing, not by a long shot, and she hated pushy people in general. But for Bobby, she'd do whatever was necessary. "What do you think about our staying tonight?"

Lacey's jaw hardened. "I'm not going to throw you out into the street right away," she said, "but you need to figure things out. Surely there's people you can call, things you can do. I don't want this to become permanent. The last thing either Buck or I needs is a stranger with a baby around here. You're poison to us right now."

Gina recoiled, shocked by the harsh words.

Buck held up a hand. "Lacey—"

"What? You know that's why you had a nightmare last night. Because she looks like Ivana and she's got a kid. It's too much for either of us."

"I'm sorry," Gina said, her heart going out to them. Underneath Lacey's brusque exterior was real pain that kept peeking through.

As for Buck, he'd looked down at his plate, but the set of his shoulders told her he wasn't happy. Something had happened to him, maybe to both of them, and Gina couldn't help wondering about it.

"I'll help this morning, if you'll allow it," she said, "and then work on doing what I can this afternoon with my car so I can move on. Maybe there's a police officer who can run me out to where it is. I'll need to take some gas."

And she'd need to rely on God, because

twenty dollars wasn't going to buy much gas or baby food, and it was all she had.

Buck heaved a sigh as he put the last stroke of paint on the breakfast-room wall. Having Gina here was even more difficult than he'd expected.

She worked hard, that was for sure. She'd single-handedly cleaned one of the guest rooms that had been finished but a mess. Carried out vinyl sheeting and masking tape, swept up nails, scrubbed the floor on her hands and knees, polished the bathroom fixtures to a shine. Now she was removing the tape from the area he'd painted yesterday.

The only time she stopped working was when Bobby cried. Then she'd slip off, he assumed to nurse the baby or to change his diaper. She'd put together a makeshift playpen from a blanket and pillows, and he crawled around it and batted at a couple of toys she had in her diaper bag.

She was resourceful, able to compartmentalize in a way few women he'd known could do. Certainly, in a way Ivana hadn't been able to do.

Unfortunately, in other ways, it was way too much like having Ivana around. Some of their best times had been working around the house together with the baby nearby. They'd felt like a happy family then.

So having Gina and Bobby here now brought back good memories, but alongside them, a keen, aching awareness of all he'd lost. All he'd thrown away, really.

He shook himself out of that line of thought. He had a mission, and he needed to stick to it. *Find out what you can about her*, Lacey had told him.

He was curious enough that the job didn't rankle. Not only would they find out whether she could be trusted to stay in their house another night, but he could maybe get rid of the crazy impression that this woman was just like Ivana.

"Do you want me to help with the trim?"

She came in now, a little out of breath, with Bobby on her hip. "Or I could work on the kitchen cabinets. I noticed they need cleaning out."

"I'd stay out of Lacey's stuff. You'd better work on the cabinets in here. Do you know how to use a screwdriver?"

"Sure."

She set Bobby up in the corner of this room and went to work washing the cabinet fronts, removing the handles, humming a wordless tune.

It was a little too domestic for him. "So, how are you gonna punt here?" he asked, his voice coming out rougher than he'd intended. "You got a plan?"

She looked up, and her eyes were dark with some emotion he couldn't name. "I thought I'd try the churches in town first," she said. "Where I lived before, some of the churches had programs for homeless families. Just until I can get on my feet and figure out what to do next." She paused. "I'd prefer finding work, but I don't know what's available."

So she thought of herself as homeless. That suggested she wasn't just traveling from point A to point B. Something else was wrong. And it was weird, because she did have that rich-girl look to her. Her clothes were stylish and new, her haircut and manicure expensive looking. But she also looked scared.

"Not sure if you'll find anything formal around here, but the churches are big on outreach. I can take you to ours. And then…you mentioned talking to the police about your car?"

"They'll want to get it off the road as much as I do." She frowned. "I just hope they won't put my name in some kind of system."

"You hiding from someone?" he asked mildly.

Her eyebrows went together and her eyes hooded. "I… Yeah. You could say that."

"Boyfriend? Husband?"

She shook her head. "I'd rather not talk about it."

That figured. A woman as pretty as she was had to have a partner, and Bobby had a father. Had someone abused her? "I'm not asking you to tell me everything, but I can help you better if I know your situation."

Her cheeks flushed with what looked like embarrassment. "Thanks." She wasn't saying more, obviously.

"Where were you headed, originally?" he pushed on as he finished painting the crown molding.

She didn't answer, so he repeated the question.

"I don't know," she said finally. "Anywhere. It didn't matter. I just had to leave." She studied the cupboard she was sanding, one of the old-fashioned and charming parts of the breakfast room, according to Lacey. "I wouldn't mind finding a place to settle for a while. As long as it was safe."

Not here, not here. He didn't need any complications in Rescue River, and this woman seemed like a complication. "Safe from what?"

She shook her head. "Too long of a story." Her voice sounded tense.

"Okay, then, what would you like to work at? What are you shooting for, jobwise?"

"My line of work was being a housewife, but obviously I need to find something else."

Hmm. From the little she'd told him, he'd guess she'd been abused. And the last thing he and Lacey needed around here was an angry husband looking for his wife and child. She didn't show any bruises, but maybe they were hidden. "What are you good at?"

"Organizing things. Raising kids. Planning parties." She shrugged. "The type of thing housewives do."

He'd have said that housewives washed dishes and cooked meals. He had a feeling about what kind of housewife she'd been— not an ordinary one. With that breakfast she'd cooked, he could imagine her catering to some wealthy husband, giving brunches for country-club ladies.

So it was very interesting that she'd run away.

Gina was bone tired after her short, broken sleep and a morning of physical work, and stressed out about the eleven messages she'd found on her phone, her in-laws demanding that she return Bobby to them immediately. Of course she'd disabled the GPS on her smartphone, but she was still worried her in-laws could somehow find her.

But Buck had offered to drive her around and, tired or not, she needed to seize the opportunity. Once she had her vehicle nearby with some gas in it, she'd feel better. She'd have an escape route and she wouldn't be quite so dependent on the kindness of strangers.

When she went out to Buck's truck, he was leaning in through the rear door, adjusting something.

"Wow, where'd you get a car seat? That's wonderful!"

He cleared his throat. "It was sitting around here." He reached out and took Bobby from her arms without meeting her eyes, then settled him into the infant seat and expertly adjusted the straps.

Mr. Tough Guy continued to surprise her.

They stopped first at the grocery store, a small, homey market a quarter the size of the superstore she'd shopped at back home. The aroma of rotisserie chicken filled the air, and bushels of produce, labeled as locally grown, stood in rows just inside the front door. Gina held Bobby in his sling, facing out so he could see the people passing by, which he loved. Buck waved to a cashier and pounded a bagger on the back as they walked toward the baby aisle.

When they got there, she picked out six jars of the cheapest baby food available. She looked over at the diapers and bit her lip, hoping the single one remaining in the diaper bag would last until she got to the box in the SUV.

Buck held a plastic basket for their purchases and studied the shelves. "Look at this stuff. Turkey with pears. What self-respecting baby would eat that?"

"I know. We used to see the weirdest baby food at World Gourmet. Avocado risotto, vanilla bean with spinach…" But that was a lifetime ago, when she'd been able to shop at the most expensive healthy foods emporium in her California town.

"Buck Armstrong, is that you?" came a woman's husky voice.

They both turned. There in the food aisle of the Star Market was the most beautiful woman Gina had ever seen. Tall, super skinny, with high cheekbones and long shiny stick-straight black hair.

A little intimidated by the woman's breathtaking looks, Gina could only offer a smile.

"Amy Franklin?" Buck reached out and hugged the woman, then held her shoulders to look at her, a genuine smile on his face. "It's been a lot of years. Welcome home!"

"It's nice to be back. Kind of." The woman wrinkled her nose. "And this must be your wife and baby! I heard you'd married. He's adorable!" She reached out to tickle Bobby's chin.

"No, I'm not—"

"No, this isn't—"

They both broke off. Bobby reached out to grab for the woman's gold necklace.

"No, sweetie." Gina loosened his fingers from the shiny chain and took a step back. "I'm just a friend he's helping," she said to the woman.

"Oh! My bad." The woman looked apologetic. "I have a little one, too," she said, turning her attention to Gina. "I'm raising my nephew, Tyler, and he's about this one's age. Maybe we could get together for a playdate sometime."

"That would be great. I'm…" She paused, wondering how to describe her uncertain status. "I'm just in from California and I don't know anyone. Well, except Buck and his sister."

"I'm originally from California, too! We should definitely get together!"

Gina felt a surge of warmth. The idea of making mom friends on her own, rather than having acquaintances who were part of her wealthy in-laws' power network, was just what she hadn't known she was hungry for. "That would be great! Where's your nephew now?"

"Oh, I'm trying out a babysitter, so I came to the grocery to give her an hour alone with him. And it's killing me! I should go back, but give me your phone number and I'll be in touch."

They punched numbers into each other's cell phones, and then the woman gave Buck a quick wave and left.

"Wow, is this town always that friendly?" she asked Buck.

He nodded and tried to smile, but his eyes were hooded and lines bracketed his mouth.

"Buck?" She touched his shoulder.

He shook his head very quickly a couple of times. "We done here?"

"Um, sure. I think so."

"Let's go." He turned and walked toward the checkout, rapid but stiff.

She hurried after him. "What just happened?"

"Nothing. I think I'll go ahead on out, wait in the truck."

"But why?"

He stopped so quickly that she ran into him. "You look a lot like my wife. My dead wife. People who don't know me well and don't know what happened are going to think you're her."

"Ooh." Realization dawned. "And your baby? What happened to your baby?"

"Dead in the same car accident." His words were clipped, toneless. "Let's go."

It was what he didn't say that haunted her

through the checkout and the ride to their next stop, the church. She longed to ask him more about it but didn't dare push the issue.

Obviously, his pain was raw. And having her around was like salt in the wound.

Too bad, because she was really starting to like Rescue River.

Chapter Three

When they arrived at the church on the edge of town, Gina was captivated. Its white steeple shone bright against the blue sky, and the building was surrounded by a grassy lawn. A creek rambled alongside the church, and several long picnic tables stood under a shelter. It was easy to picture small-town church picnics on that lawn.

Gina hoisted Bobby to her hip and followed Buck toward the church. As they walked up the steps, the door opened and several men came out dressed in work clothes, followed by another in a police uniform. Everyone greeted Buck, and the police officer tickled Bobby under his chin, making him giggle. That close, Gina could see the name tag that indicated he was the chief. Her stomach tightened. For the first time in her life, she felt like law enforcement officers were her enemies, not her friends.

Buck introduced her and briefly explained her story, even though Gina was willing him to be quiet with all her silent might.

"Car broke down, eh?" Chief Dion said. "SUV? White?"

"That's the one," she said faintly.

"Saw it this morning. Ran the plates."

Gina's heart thudded like a doom-filled drumbeat. Had her in-laws reported her car missing?

"Our computers aren't communicating too well with those in California, so I couldn't get any information," he said. "Glad to know it's got an owner. Need any help getting back on the road?"

"It's just out of—"

"We might," Buck interjected. "We're headed out there in just a few minutes."

"Call me if there's any problem," Chief Dion offered. "In fact, I might be able to meet you out there or have one of our officers meet you. Make sure everything's okay."

"Sounds good."

As soon as Dion was gone, she turned to Buck. "Why'd you tell him we might need help? It's just out of gas. And I'd...rather not have police involvement."

"Oh? Why's that?"

"It's complicated." He'd been very helpful, and yet she couldn't fully trust him. She'd yet to meet the person who couldn't be swayed by her in-laws' money and power. The police detective she'd consulted privately about their unnecessary roughness had brushed aside her concerns and seemed more interested in how to get the wealthy couple to donate even more money to the local police department.

No, it was her and Bobby against the world.

She headed on into the church, welcoming the dark, cool air.

"Come on—pastor's this way." As he took the lead, his shoulder brushed against her in the narrow hallway. An awareness clicked into her, something she hadn't felt since well before her husband had died. Whoa. What was *that*?

As they approached a doorway marked Pastor's Study, a middle-aged man stood up from behind the desk and came out to greet them, shaking Buck's hand heartily and then turning to her. "What a pleasure! Buck, we don't see you here often enough these days. You just missed the men's prayer group, fixing up one of the elementary classrooms. What brings you here?"

"This is Gina," Buck said. "She's looking for some help. Gina, meet Pastor Ricky."

Heat flushed Gina's face. She hated being in this position: helpless, homeless, asking for what amounted to a handout. *It's for Bobby*, she reminded herself.

The pastor invited them in, and Gina sat down, cuddled Bobby to her chest and explained their situation to a minimal degree. Homeless, purse stolen, looking for work and a place to stay.

The pastor nodded sympathetically. "The church isn't really set up for that," he said. "When we need places for people to stay, we usually ask families to put them up. In fact, Lacey, Buck's sister, has helped us out a few times."

"It would work better if she stayed somewhere else," Buck said.

Ouch! Gina had been an interloper back at her in-laws' place, where she'd been tolerated because she had given birth to the heir to the empire. But that feeling of always being on the outside, a burden, was a part of what she'd been fleeing.

The last thing she wanted was to feel that way at Lacey's place, but Buck was making it obvious that he didn't want her there.

"Let's see. There's Lou Ann Miller, but I

think she's away visiting her sister. Maybe Susan Hayashi? Except her mom and brother are here visiting, and they're doing some renovations on Sam's house. Getting ready for the wedding, you know. Such a nice couple." He looked at Buck's impatient expression and waved a hand. "But you don't need to hear about all that. You're sure Lacey's place isn't an option?"

"Like I said, somewhere else would be better."

"Sure enough. I'll ask around. And I'll check the balance in the emergency fund." The pastor studied Buck with a level expression, obviously wondering what was going on. "I'd take you in myself, except we have a houseful of teenagers for the Artists for Christ Concert over in Mansfield. Not very quiet for your baby."

As if on cue, Bobby wiggled hard, trying to get down to the floor, and she gave the place a quick check for hazards and then set him down. "Do you know of any jobs?" she blurted out before she knew what she was saying. And wondered when Rescue River had become a viable place to live. "I don't want charity—I want to work, and I'm willing to do anything. I'm good at decorating, cooking and event planning, and I'm really organized. And I have most of a college degree." Her voice cracked a little on the last word. She'd been thinking about her job skills ever since she left her in-laws' place, and figuring out how to package her housewife background into something more impressive. Still, it was hard to brag about herself.

"Hmm. Again, we're a very small town, so I don't know of much. But what about Lacey? She's doing all that renovation. Surely she could use some help…"

"That's not going to work." Buck's words were flat, firm and final.

And that irked Gina. She scooped Bobby back up into her arms. "I'm sorry I remind you of your ex. I'll get out of your hair as soon as I can. But I have to do my best for my son. Why are you so against my working for Lacey, if I can talk her into it?"

He lifted an eyebrow, clearly trying to play it cool. "Because you're on the run and we know nothing about you." He rubbed the back of his neck with one hand. "And…look, Lacey's not as strong as she acts. Let's leave it at that."

What could she say? She nodded, feeling like there was more to the story.

The pastor put a hand on each of their arms. "Let's take it to the Lord," he suggested, and Gina felt ashamed she hadn't done more praying about her situation. She'd been too tired and too worried, but that was exactly when she needed to turn it over to God. Buck and Gina bowed their heads, and the pastor uttered a short prayer for Gina to find shelter and work and for everyone to get along. Something like that. Though she felt too upset and flustered to focus on the words, the pastor's heartfelt prayer offered a tiny sense of peace.

At the gas station, Buck pulled out a couple of five-gallon gas cans. "We'll fill both of these," he said to the attendant who came out to help, even though they were at a self-serve pump.

Gina touched Buck's arm, embarrassed. "Um, could we just fill one? About halfway? That should do me until..." She trailed off, her face heating. Never in her life had she been completely broke, not able to afford more than a couple of gallons of gas at a time.

He waved a hand. "Don't worry about it. We'll fill both."

"No, I'd rather just do what I can afford."

"I said don't worry about it."

"Trying to get me as far away as you can, are you?" She was half joking, and then she saw on his face that she'd guessed exactly right. "Fine, fill both." She slammed back into Buck's truck, feeling unaccountably hurt.

There was no particular reason why Buck should like her or want her to stay. Just because he'd rescued her last night, he didn't have responsibility for her future or Bobby's. That was solely on her shoulders.

The thing was, as she rode around Rescue River, even now as she watched the gasstation attendant clap Buck on the shoulder and help him lift the heavy gas cans into the back of his pickup, she *liked* this place. She could picture herself and Bobby playing in the park and attending the church and getting together with other friendly people. She could imagine herself a part of this community.

On the other hand, the idea of the man beside her resisting every moment of her presence was disconcerting. She hated not being wanted. She'd grown up feeling that way, and she'd married into a family where she felt like an outsider. Was she continuing her same sick pattern?

Rescue River was where the Lord had led

her. It seemed like the perfect place to stay, at least for a while.

She just had to convince Buck not to block the whole idea.

Buck helped Gina fill the gas tank on her loaded, late-model SUV, continuing to wonder what her story was, continuing to get distracted by the lemony scent of her hair. Dion was there, too, helping and subtly questioning, observing everything.

It was early evening, but Buck could still hear the steady *chink-chink-chink* of a rotary tiller off in the distance. Probably Rob Richardson, trying to get his field finished before the rain came on. Sun peeked through a bank of dark clouds, illuminating the freshly plowed acre beside them. Buck inhaled the sweet, pungent zing that indicated a storm was headed their way.

Gina thanked them both politely, strapped Bobby into the car seat and headed back to the guesthouse. Buck was about to climb into his truck when Dion gestured to him. "Stay back a minute, would you?"

Buck turned toward the police chief. "Sure. What's up?"

It wasn't like he was eager to get home. He was half hoping that Gina, now that she had a tank of gas and some baby food, would hightail it to the next town. Or the next state.

Then again, what would she do if she left Rescue River? Alone without money and with a baby to care for, what were the odds that she'd survive, let alone do well?

He didn't want to worry about her, because being around her disturbed him on so many levels. Her resemblance to Ivana evoked all kinds of feelings he'd had during his marriage. That initial attraction. Anger at how Ivana's love for him had cooled. Fear that he'd made a lifelong mistake in marrying her, and guilt that he'd let his feelings show.

Horrible guilt about how everything had

ended. And with that, the way his drinking had spiraled out of control.

"We have a little bit of a problem," Dion said.

"With the car?"

"More so with the baby. Did you notice the bandage on his arm?"

Buck nodded. "She said it's a scratch."

"Mmm-hmm. Have you seen any other marks on the kid?"

Buck stared at Dion as the puzzle pieces started moving into place. "You're thinking... what? That somebody abused the baby?"

"Could be." Dion nodded, not looking at Buck, staring out over the fields. "Could be her."

"No." Buck reeled back against that accusation. "I've seen how protective she is. She wouldn't do anything to hurt him. I more got the impression that she's running away."

"That's my gut instinct, too, but she's a pretty woman and a mother, so guys like us can be a little distracted. Keep your eyes open for it, would you?"

"Did you find out something against her?"

Dion frowned. "Not officially. But I have a few friends in law enforcement on the West Coast. Apparently, someone tried to report the car stolen, only to find out that it's not even eligible for unlawful use for another four days."

"Unlawful use? So…"

"So she took a car that belongs to a family member or friend. Maybe she had permission to use it, but not to take off in it."

"What are you saying? What do you want to do?"

"I'm thinking she's either a woman in trouble, or she's trouble herself. Either way, that baby's the victim."

"So we should…"

"We should try to get her to stay in Rescue River, is what I'm thinking." Dion frowned, rubbed a hand over his chin. "No, it's not exactly our problem, and we can't make her stay, but it would be a good thing for her to stick around here until I can make some phone calls, find out what her story is. It's safe here, and I can monitor the situation, make sure she's not the abuser and maybe prevent those who are from finding her."

Something primal raised the hairs on the back of Buck's neck, and he gave Dion a narrow stare. "You like her, don't you?"

They weren't exactly friends. Dion had pulled Buck out of a couple of fights in his role as a cop, when Buck was drinking. Nowadays, Dion was more likely to evangelize him, which was almost worse. But at least it meant that Dion didn't think he was unredeemable, like so many in town did.

Maybe they had the beginnings of a friendship, but it wasn't enough to quell Buck's irrational twinge of jealousy at the thought of Dion liking Gina.

Dion's eyebrows came together. "What're you talking about, man? I don't even know her. I just see a Christian duty, and a judicial one, to watch out for her. And to watch her. Asking for your help as a citizen."

Buck chuckled, feeling relieved. "That's a first. You asking me to help you on the right side of the law."

"People change." Dion gave him a level stare. "Remember that, my man. People change."

Buck pondered that thought all the way home, and it gave him a spring to his step as he trotted up the guesthouse stairs, trying to stay ahead of the rain that was starting to fall. People changed. Maybe even him.

Just before he touched the door handle, he saw a movement on the far side of the porch.

Gina. Rocking gently on the porch swing, pulling a blanket over her shoulder, probably to shield Bobby from the sound of Buck's footsteps and the flash of lightning.

He walked quietly toward them, mindful of what Dion had said. He wanted to watch how she handled Bobby with Dion's questions in mind. If Gina was in trouble, he wanted to help her somehow. He couldn't push her away, no matter how disturbing it was to be around her. She could be in real danger.

"Hey," he said, keeping his concerns out of his tone. "You made it back okay? Vehicle's running well?"

She nodded. "Yes, and Lacey said we can stay one more night. Only one, though. Then we have to be on our way." She sounded sad.

"Do you…want to stay more?"

She adjusted Bobby with a tender care and private, loving smile. Then she looked out at the rainy twilight. "I like it here, and it feels safe. Like a good place to get my bearings."

"That's the town's history and reputation," he said. "Rescue River's always opened its arms to those in need."

"It feels welcoming." She shot him a glance. "Well, mostly."

Buck decided to be honest. "I feel for your situation, but…" He trailed off as she adjusted Bobby again, and he realized exactly what she was doing.

She was nursing him.

He stood up quickly. "Whoa, I'm sorry to intrude. I didn't realize…"

"It's okay," she said, chuckling. "It's a natural thing and I know how to cover up. I've fed Bobby in all kinds of places."

"That's…pretty cool." He'd never been one of those guys who was turned off by nursing or pregnancy or childbirth. Just the opposite, in fact. He'd never loved Ivana more, never felt closer to her, than when she was in the height and glory of womanhood, pregnant with his child or feeding little Mia from her own body. The whole thing amazed him. God's creativity in action.

Rain was pounding hard now, bringing with it a fresh, clean-washed smell and cooler air.

He felt himself looking at Gina in a new light. His heart warmed toward her in a visceral way: that ancient male reaction to a mother and child in need. Yes, having her here was disturbing, but he thought he could handle it, at least for a short time.

And after all, he wouldn't be here for long himself. He was putting every penny he had into making restitution, repaying money he'd borrowed, getting back on his feet. Living here with Lacey rent-free in exchange for his renovation work. He didn't have the means to leave town, not yet, but he would soon.

"I like it here, Buck," Gina said. "I think God may have sent me and Bobby here for a reason. I'm thinking, maybe, I'd like to stay."

His ambivalence must have shown on his face, because she cocked her head to one side and spoke. "That bothers you, doesn't it? How come? Is it about my resemblance to your wife?"

"Somewhat." Actually, he was starting to wonder how he'd ever mistaken her for Ivana. She had a plucky strength and determination, a set to her chin, a way of holding herself that were completely her own. Still, he had questions.

She frowned and looked down at Bobby, who was starting to show signs of being done nursing. She turned a little away and wiped his mouth.

"Want me to burp him?" he asked before he could stop himself.

She quirked an eyebrow. "Can you?"

"Sure." He leaned down and picked up the baby boy and held him against his shoulder. He was sturdier than Mia had been. Gina had mentioned that Bobby was ten months. Mia had made it only eight.

But propping a baby with one hand, flipping the burp cloth over his shoulder, patting the baby's back, that all came right back to him. Like riding a bike. You didn't forget.

He pulled Bobby a little closer, breathing him in, cherishing the feel of the baby, pretending he was Mia. Pretending his little daughter was still alive and well and happy. That he hadn't driven Ivana from their home in a moment of anger and desperation.

If only none of it had happened.

"Look," she said, "I'm sorry if I bring up memories for you. Maybe I'll get on my feet quickly and be able to get out of here. But meanwhile..."

"Meanwhile what?" He was holding her baby in the rainy twilight, looking at her and finding her beautiful, and feeling like he might be stepping into the biggest mess of his life.

And then, as he adjusted the sweet little bundle in his arms, Bobby's pajama leg came up and he saw it.

A bruise the size of a beer coaster. Or a man's fist.

"If it were just me, I'd leave for your sake," she said. "But this looks like the perfect safe place for Bobby, and I have to put him first."

He concealed his reaction to the bruise and stroked the baby's downy hair, his heart pounding. "Of course you do."

"But I don't know why I'm even talking to you about it. Your sister's the one who's determined to get rid of me." She was looking up at him with troubled eyes as the wind blew a strand of hair in front of her face. "I don't know what to do."

He could see that it cost her to admit that, to ask for advice. She'd do it, though, for her son. He could already tell she was that kind of woman.

He didn't think she could possibly have injured Bobby, which meant that someone else had done it. Someone she was running from?

And if so, what right did he have to push her away? Especially if it resulted in this little one being hurt again?

He patted Bobby's back until a loud burp made them both laugh. Then he sat down in the rocker across from the porch swing, still holding Bobby.

"Want to tell me about Bobby's father?"

She drew in a breath and let it out again, slowly, seeming to consider. Finally, she spoke. "Hank was…smart and handsome. And rich."

He smiled. "Bodes well for Bobby."

"Yes. I just hope he doesn't inherit a couple of the other genes."

"Like?"

"Like the addiction-prone one."

"Oh." Buck looked away, feeling ashamed. Addiction was considered genetic by some, but more of a character flaw by most. And it was a flaw he shared. "Did your husband ever do AA or anything like that?"

"He was more into cocaine," she said, "but sure, he did NA. Plenty of times."

"It never took?" That was discouraging. "You're talking about him in the past tense. Is he dead?"

"He died not long after Bobby was born. Ski accident."

"Drugs?"

She nodded. "Yes. He was high, skiing one of the most dangerous double black diamond slopes in California. He didn't have a chance."

"I'm sorry." Why did a guy do drugs when he had a wife and baby who needed him?

Then again, why did any addict do what he did?

"So that's not who you're running from."

She shook her head. "No. It's…my in-laws."

"Your husband's family? What's the problem there?"

She sighed. "Abuse, if you must know. I don't want to talk about it."

Buck's pulse rate shot up. There it was. He'd like to get his hands on those people. "If they abused you or Bobby, they should go to prison."

"They should, but they won't," she said with complete certainty.

"They're that powerful?"

"They're that powerful."

The sky was black velvet now, the air cooling more. She huddled under the blanket she'd been using as a nursing cover. She looked so pretty. So vulnerable. So in need of protection.

As was the little baby now sleeping in his arms.

He wasn't going to let anything happen between him and Gina, no way, but he had to let her stay. Dion had asked him to, and he had a lot to report to the police chief. And maybe, just maybe, it was a way for him to get over Ivana, move on. Maybe this was part of the restitution he was trying to practice in his recovery.

He was to make amends for wrongs he had done. Well, he was doing that with bar owners around town, with friends he'd borrowed from. With Lacey, who'd had to put up with a lot from him during his two-year drinking spree.

But the people he'd wronged the most were dead.

Could he make restitution through Gina and Bobby? Give something to them, and that way right the balance with his wife and child, who were beyond earthly help?

And once he'd made his restitution and saved up a little money, he'd leave. Leave, with a clean slate, and start over somewhere

where nobody knew his past. It was what he wanted. All he wanted. All he was working for.

The wind blew the cool farm air toward the house, fragrant with fresh-plowed earth. Crickets sang out in a chorus. Streetlights flickered on down the block, where the shops were.

He slid one hand away from the baby and into his pocket where he carried his recovery coin. Six months sober. He could handle this new challenge.

"I'll talk to Lacey," he said gruffly. "Try to get her to let you stay awhile. And you can work on the renovation with me."

Chapter Four

Later that night, Gina had just closed her eyes when her phone buzzed. She grabbed it, not wanting to risk waking Bobby.

When she saw it was her friend Haley, back in California, she sat upright. "Hang on," she whispered and slipped a robe over her light-weight tank top and shorts.

Grabbing her phone, she hurried down to the small alcove on the landing of the stairs. It was one of the few public areas in the guesthouse that was finished, with lace curtains and a braided rug. She settled into the window seat, pulled her feet up underneath her and leaned back against comfortable cushions. She could see the half-open door of her room at the top of the stairs, so she'd notice if Bobby stirred.

"Okay, I can talk," she said quietly. "How are you? I miss you so much!" Ever since she and Haley had shared a room on the maternity floor, their babies born within hours of one another, they'd been close friends. Haley was the only person in whom Gina had confided about her plans to leave town.

"I miss you, too, but that's not why I called."

"Are the dogs okay?"

Haley laughed. "They're bad, and spoiled, but you know I love them. No, that's not the problem."

"Did you find anything out?" She was hoping, though not expecting, that Haley had figured out a way she could gain access to some of the money she should have inherited as Hank's widow.

"It's not good news." Haley cleared her throat and went into business mode, not a problem for her since she worked in a bank. "I've been nosing around, and it sounds like assets in probate can be tangled up for a year, eighteen months if the estate is complicated."

"Which it is." Hank's parents, seeing the mess Hank had made of his life after Bobby was born, had put most of his inheritance in trust. Gina even suspected that they'd gotten Hank to sign some CDs over to them when he was high.

"I talked to my manager—in confidence, didn't identify you—and she said that because there wasn't a will, there's no way around this long process. I'm so mad Hank didn't protect you and Bobby!"

"I know." Gina's chest ached, as it always did when she thought of Hank. He'd been so much fun when they'd first met; he'd swept her off her feet, had loved her madly. In the first two years of their marriage she'd realized his partying went further than it should—sometimes much further—

but they'd still had a base of love and care for each other.

Bobby's arrival had changed everything. The responsibility of fatherhood had overwhelmed Hank, and Gina, sleep deprived and cranky, hadn't been as understanding as before. He'd gone off the deep end, dug into his bad habits and made the leap from recreational drug user to addict.

"He wasn't thinking straight," she said to Haley and left it at that.

"The good news is, within a few years, when it's all straightened out, you and Bobby should be okay." Haley's voice didn't sound all that reassuring, though.

"It sounds like there's a *but* in there somewhere."

"There is." Haley's voice sounded shaky. "Gina, there's a big problem."

"What? Tell me." Gina's heart felt like a stone. She wanted to start a new life, for herself but even more, for Bobby. But right now, it seemed like she'd never get free.

"It's your in-laws. When I saw Hank's cousin this morning, she told me they're going to report your car as stolen."

"What?" From the downstairs kitchen, Gina heard what sounded like an argument and lowered her voice. "That car's mine! Hank gave it to me!"

"But is the title in your name?"

Gina squeezed her eyes shut as if she could block out this unwelcome news. "No. It was in Hank's name."

"And since the estate's stuck in probate…"

Gina leaned her head back against the window, staring up at the ceiling. If they'd reported the car stolen, she was essentially a common criminal.

"Gina? Honey?"

Gina blew out a breath. "I'll be tracked down for sure, then, because the police department here has my vehicle information. What am I going to do?" Her voice broke on the last couple of words, and she swallowed hard, determined to maintain control.

"I've already thought about that. You've got to give it back, that's all."

"Give it back? When I'm here and they're in California?"

"Yep, and I've figured out how. You use one of those driving services. They load your vehicle on a truck and drive it across the country. It's done all the time."

Gina was still wrapping her mind around the facts: that her car wasn't her car, and that she was a wanted criminal. "It's got to be expensive," she said finally. "I'm almost out of money."

"Didn't you say you had a debit card?"

She did. "But it's not safe to use it." It wasn't as if there was a lot of money in the old joint account—Hank had drained most of it away in the months before his death—but there was something. Something for Bobby's future, if they could make it through the first couple of months.

Haley sighed audibly. "No. No, it's not safe,

especially now that you're a wanted person. The police could track you to where you are."

Gina felt a sharp rush of shame that she had no savings of her own. If only she hadn't acquiesced to staying home with Bobby... She glanced up toward her room. No, she couldn't regret that decision. They'd both agreed that since they had the means, it would be best for her to spend Bobby's early years at home with him.

She shoved open the window, letting the rain-soaked breeze soothe her hot face.

"We've got to hire you a transportation service, have you send back the car. The way I see it, you don't have a choice." Haley cleared her throat. "I talked to Josh. We...we can pay for it."

"No." Gina couldn't let her friend do that. She and her husband had tons of student debt and no family money. Although they both worked, the high cost of living in their part of the state made it so that they barely scraped by every month.

And yet Haley was right. Staying out of trouble with the law was a bigger priority even than a financial safety net.

"Look, what if I mail you my ATM card? That way you can take the money out of my account, and if it's traced, it'll be local, not here." Gina couldn't believe how quickly she was able to flip into criminal mode when it was Bobby's safety in question. "If I do that, can you set it up for me? Do we just send the SUV to them? I'm afraid they'll find out where it came from and track us down."

"Nope. Overnight the card to me, and I'll get it all set up right away. As soon as the SUV arrives, I'll drive it over to your in-laws' place and leave it."

"How? In the middle of the night?"

"Maybe. Or maybe I'll figure out some explanation." She paused. "I really want this to work for you, Gina. I miss you, but you did the right thing. Bobby comes first."

"Thank you so much. You're an amazing

friend." Her throat tight, she chatted for a couple more minutes and then ended the call.

How was she going to manage without a vehicle? And yet, what choice did she have?

She looked out the window at the street-lights of Rescue River. The main street glistened with today's rain. She could see the market, the diner, the library.

She could see them, which meant she could walk to them. She looked up at the stars. "You knew what You were doing when You put me here, Father," she murmured in a low voice.

She let out a sigh and slid her feet down to the floor...only to shriek at the sight of a large figure standing a couple of steps down from the landing. When she recognized Buck, her heart rate settled a little.

He flicked on the hall light. "Sorry to startle you. I was talking to Lacey about your situation. Coming upstairs to my room." Unnecessarily, he gestured toward the upper floor. "I didn't mean to eavesdrop."

She remembered the raised voices she'd heard. "Let me guess," she said. "Your talk with Lacey didn't go well."

"I'm afraid not." He sat on the other end of the curved window seat, his face barely visible in the glow of a streetlight. "She's just not comfortable having you here. She said you could stay for a couple more days, through Monday, Tuesday if you really need to, but that's all."

The weight of her responsibilities pressed down on Gina. She couldn't stay, then, not unless she found another job. But she couldn't go, not with her transportation being taken out from under her.

"Hey, I'm sorry." He reached out a hand and patted her shoulder.

Surely he meant it as a friendly touch, but to Gina, the warmth of his large hand made her want to hurl herself into his arms. He seemed so strong and competent and kind.

And she couldn't give in to that desire to

be rescued. "Thanks for trying. With God's help, I'll figure out something."

Rather than nodding and moving away, he gave her shoulder another pat and looked into her eyes. "When I met you, I thought you were one of those ladies who lunch, someone who never had a problem. But that's far from the truth, isn't it?"

"Miles away." She couldn't handle the compassion in his eyes, but she couldn't look away, either.

"If I wasn't knee-deep in problems of my own, problems of my own creation, I'd try to help you more." He squeezed her shoulder once and then pulled his hand away.

"Thanks." She actually believed him.

"One thing I *can* offer," he said, "is an invitation to church tomorrow. Nine o'clock. It's a great community church, the one we stopped by before, and who knows, maybe someone is hiring or can put you up." He sounded doubtful. And she couldn't tell whether he wanted her to stay or not. Probably not.

He was offering her solace, and shamefully, church didn't seem like a lot of help right now. But it was what she had, and she knew, intellectually at least, that God was big enough to handle any problem.

And she also knew that staying here in the dim moonlight, talking to a very handsome and compassionate man, wasn't the solution to anything. She stood and turned toward the stairs. "I'd love to go. Thanks for asking."

Minutes after Gina went into her room and closed the door, Buck trotted downstairs. He was putting on his coat when Lacey came out of the kitchen, holding her orange cat in her arms.

"Where are you going?" she asked. "It's late."

"Need some air." The conversation with Gina had thrown him off balance in more ways than one, and he knew he wouldn't sleep anytime soon.

Not to mention he was worried about the baby. Earlier tonight, when Gina had gone inside to fetch his binky, Buck had snapped a photo of Bobby's bruise to show Dion.

His sister cuddled the cat closer and studied him, her forehead wrinkled.

"It's just a walk, Lace."

"You're sure?"

"Yes!" Then, ashamed of his sharp tone, he put an arm around her shoulders and gave her a gentle squeeze. He shouldn't be mad at her when she'd bailed him out of so many problems. Between her own tragedies and his bad behavior, his waiflike younger sister had been forced to grow stronger than any woman should have to be. "I won't be out long and I won't do…what I used to do."

"I know." She leaned into his side. "I just got in the habit of worrying about you, know what I mean?"

"I know. But I'm fine."

At least, he *hoped* he was fine, he thought as he stepped out the door. In the past, he'd have for sure gone on a bender just because he felt mixed up about that encounter with Gina.

He was worried about what he'd overheard, but that wasn't all of it.

Turned out God had a sense of humor. He was *attracted* to the pretty, maternal stranger.

Buck blew out a sigh and strode through Rescue River's small business district. A farming community to the core, the town shut down early. The diner and the shops all had doors closed and lights off.

Clouds scuttled over the moon and a breeze rattled the tree limbs. Buck pulled his coat closer around him. Ohio weather. Yesterday had been springlike, but tonight it felt like a front was coming through.

There *was* one business still open, one place where light and happy noises indicated life: the Ace Tavern.

Buck straightened his back and told himself to keep walking. And he did. He walked past.

Behind him, the door of the tavern opened. Could he be blamed for turning back? Any combat vet worth his salt had it ingrained: know what's going on behind you.

A long-haired woman came out, alone. Wearing a jacket that didn't look too warm, skintight jeans and ridiculously high heels. There was a click, a flash, and she got her cigarette lit, then looked up and saw him. "Hey, handsome, come buy me a drink," she said. Then she squinted and leaned toward him, catching herself on the bar's wooden outside wall. "Well, if you ain't a sight for sore eyes. Buck Armstrong."

He stepped closer and recognition dawned. "Hey, Heather, how's it going?" He reached out to grasp her hand and ended up steadying her. "Been a while." Heather was at least fifteen years older than Buck, but they'd been good drinking buddies. Heather was one of the few people in town who'd been able to match Buck shot for shot.

The thought of that brought a tight feeling to his throat.

A glass of whiskey, he knew, would take that feeling away. Warm him right up, too.

"Gonna finish my smoke and then go back in. C'mon, have a cold one and let me know what you been up to." She spoke slowly and carefully but still tripped over a few of the words. Did he used to sound like that?

"You planning on driving home tonight?" He knew Heather lived out in the country, had been to a couple of parties at her place.

"Sure, yeah. Why, want to come out my way?"

"No, not tonight, thanks."

"Your loss." She turned to go back into the bar and stumbled.

Catching her, Buck blew out a breath. He knew well enough what falling-down drunk looked like, and Heather was falling-down drunk. And he needed to make sure someone would take care of her. Holding her elbow, he steered her inside.

The bar wasn't crowded. A couple of guys playing pool, a man and woman talking intently in a booth, and three or four of his old acquaintances at the bar. Regulars, people who didn't have much family. Whether they hung out at the Ace because of that, or whether their drinking had pushed loved ones away, they didn't have another place to go, and the bar served as home to them.

"Hey, Armstrong!" Word circled around the place, and it was like he'd never left. Guys clapping him on the back, Heather clinging to his arm, proud to have brought in a popular old friend, the bartender turning over glasses, shot and a beer, his old favorite.

"Not tonight, Arnie," he told the bartender, leading Heather to a table and then extricating himself from her grasp.

Mild catcalls of disapproval greeted his refusal. Everyone here knew he was in AA and probably didn't want to tempt him too badly, but they'd welcome him back into the fold in a minute. His choice.

He stepped over to the bar and handed Arnie a couple of bills. "Get someone to take Heather home tonight, could you? She shouldn't be driving."

Arnie pocketed the money with a smile. "I'll take her myself."

"Thanks." *Get out of here, now.* He looked around at the beer signs, the glittering rows of bottles, ran a hand over the scarred wooden bar. This place had been here forever. A classic.

Get out now.

He turned toward the door.

"Sure I can't get you a drink? My treat." Arnie held up a glass.

Get out. Buck fingered his sobriety coin, squeezed it hard until the edges dug into his palm. Looked up at the ceiling, made a plea.

"No. No, thank you." Somehow, he got his mouth to form the words and got his feet to start marching. Like marching during wartime, when you'd been up twenty-four hours and more and didn't think your legs could carry you. One step at a time.

A moment later he was out of the bar and leaning against the wooden front of it, breathing hard. He pulled out his sobriety coin and, in the light from the bar's window, read the serenity prayer printed in tiny letters on the back. Or pretended to read it; actually, he knew it by heart. *God, grant me the serenity to accept the things I cannot change, the courage to...*

In front of him, a police cruiser stopped, and he was still enough of a drunk that his heart raced before he remembered he hadn't done anything wrong.

Dion stepped out and walked over, stood a little closer than was polite. Undoubtedly trying to tell if Buck smelled of liquor. "In trouble, my friend?"

"Just got away from it." He held up his coin.

Dion narrowed his eyes, studying it, and

then the light dawned. "Your recovery coin. Close call?"

Buck nodded, his heart rate settling back to normal. The fresh, cold air braced him. He could do this.

He hoped.

"Want to grab a cup of coffee? I'm done with my shift."

He *wanted* a drink. But no. He didn't intend to go back there, not ever. "Thanks—coffee sounds good," he said and got into the cruiser.

He'd definitely have something to share at tomorrow's AA meeting.

When they reached the truckers' restaurant out by the highway—the only nondrinking place open at this hour—the owner hurried toward them. He was a short man in a white shirt with pants pulled up high on his ample belly, and his hand was raised like a stop sign. "You're welcome, Chief, but him I won't serve."

Heat rose in Buck's face. He dimly remembered some late-night, postbar confrontation, some shouting, a few shoves.

The smells of coffee and fried food wafted through the air. A couple of uniformed waitresses stood near the cash register, watching. They probably remembered Buck, too, and not in a good way.

He turned to go.

"He's my guest," Dion said. His voice was quiet, but he'd drawn himself up tall. He was a big man, and commanding, and the restaurant manager visibly cringed.

"Well, all right, if you'll take full responsibility. But if there's any trouble…"

"If there's trouble, I'll handle it, my friend."

The manager nodded and stepped aside, and Dion led the way to a booth in the restaurant's back corner.

Once they'd both ordered coffee, Buck let his head sink onto one fist and stared down at the none-too-clean table. "I'll never get out from under my reputation. I've got to leave Rescue River. Repay my debts and leave."

Dion shook his head, slowly. "You're a new creation. Did you think that was just words?"

"The outside looks the same, and no one around here believes in the change. It's dangerous," he added for clarification, remembering Arnie holding up the glass.

Instead of responding to that, Dion studied him. "What was it had you out walking so late?"

Buck looked at Dion's dark eyes, eyes that seemed to hold a depth of thought and wisdom beyond most of the people Buck knew. "Did you ever meet a woman you really liked, but you knew she was out of reach?"

Dion's mouth twisted a little and he looked out across the restaurant. "In a manner of speaking."

Daisy Hinton, the town's pretty blonde social worker, sprang into Buck's mind. He'd heard the rumors about her and Dion but didn't know whether there was any substance to them.

Dion rubbed the back of his neck. "What

are we talking about here? You got a crush on someone unattainable?"

Buck sighed. "It's Gina. I like her."

"The new lady in town?" Dion lifted an eyebrow. "Back up, my man. What have you heard? How's the baby doing?"

"The good news is, Bobby is doing fine. Gina couldn't possibly be the one who was abusing him. He's thriving, and she's real gentle with him."

"Good." Dion sipped at his hot coffee. "What's the bad news?"

Buck hesitated. Should he tell Dion what he'd overheard, possibly getting Gina into trouble? But if he didn't tell Dion, and something happened to her that could have been prevented…

"I can tell you know something," Dion said, "so why don't you go on and tell me."

Buck shook his head. "Man, I feel sorry for your kids, if you ever have any. You're going to read them like a book."

A strange expression crossed Dion's face

so quickly that Buck decided he must have imagined it. He stirred sugar into his coffee. "It was just a little something I overheard. One-sided phone conversation."

Dion lifted an eyebrow, waiting.

"She was talking about whether she and Bobby could be hunted down here. Something about mailing an ATM card to a friend so the withdrawal couldn't be traced." He paused, then added, "She also sounded worried about the fact that you have her vehicle information. And it sounds like she's going to ship her car back to California."

Dion's eyes narrowed. "So the vehicle *was* stolen."

"I thought so, too. But she seems to want to give it back."

Dion shook his head, a mirthless chuckle escaping. "That's what they all say."

"She wasn't saying it to make an impression. She was talking to a friend."

"And…there's nothing illegal about shipping a car. But if she doesn't have the registration or title or some identifying paperwork, no legitimate shipper will take it on."

"So we could just wait and see. If she's able to ship the car, that means she's got the rights to it."

"Or something." Dion frowned. "Tell you what. I'll do a little digging, but I'm not going to bring a lady in for wanting to ship a car. What I *am* going to do is to keep a pretty close eye on her."

Buck nodded. Dion had to do his job. And thinking of that reminded him of the photo he'd taken. "Look at this," he said as he pulled out his phone and brought up the image. "Zoom in on the baby's leg."

Dion's eyebrows rose. "Is that a bruise?"

Buck nodded and held up a hand. "After seeing her with the baby, there's no way she could be at fault. She's very protective of him. Protective like someone who's escaping an abuser, not someone who's an abuser herself."

Dion's brows drew together. "Maybe."

"Give her a chance," Buck said. "She could be a new creation, too."

"Touché, my man. But my job is to clean up the messes people make along the way." He leveled a pointed gaze at Buck. "And your job is to stay sober and help your sister. Not to get overinvolved with a pretty possible criminal passing through town."

"You warning me?"

"Let's just say we're not that far removed from the days I had to pull you out of that bar and toss you in jail to sober up. Worst thing a former drinker can do is to get involved with the wrong company."

Buck nodded, but he couldn't truly agree with Dion. He had the distinct feeling that he, with his miserable track record, was the wrong company for Gina. Not the other way around.

Chapter Five

Gina found the next day's church service renewing and refreshing, and afterward, friendly people talked her into attending the church luncheon and meeting to plan the Freedom Festival. After a quick check on Bobby, who was loving the church nursery, she found her way to the fellowship hall.

Amy, the tall, gorgeous woman she'd met in the grocery store with Buck, hurried over. "Hey, they're just finishing up the general meeting, and everyone's going to eat before breaking into committees. You should come sit next to me and we can talk about getting our babies together."

"That would be nice." Although she feared she wouldn't find a way to stay in Rescue River long enough to build real friendships, Gina was grateful to be able to sit with someone other than Buck and Lacey. She didn't want to impose on them.

After she'd gotten her plate of meat loaf, mashed potatoes and green beans, she headed over to where Amy was gesturing. And sighed. Amy was next to Buck and Lacey at a table full of people. So Gina ended up sitting with them after all.

Conversation focused on the upcoming festival. Apparently, it had been going on for years, celebrating Rescue River's history with the Underground Railroad and the arrival of spring, which had meant easier travel for those seeking freedom.

Lacey was more animated today, talking about the guesthouse. "There's a room in the basement and another in the attic that were kept available for fugitive slaves. Apparently, at one time there were thirty people staying at the house."

"You should get a historic-landmark designation!" Gina said. "It's a lot of paperwork, but with a history like that, I'm sure you'd be approved."

Lacey didn't seem to hear her, speaking instead to Amy about how hard it was to get the renovation done while working full-time.

"I could help you with it," Gina offered when there was a break in the conversation. "At least to get it on the National Register of Historic Places, which is easier. I've helped a couple of organizations do it."

Lacey gave her a look, one Gina could read. It was the same look she'd gotten when she'd tried to connect with the popular girls back in high school. *You don't belong*, it said.

Gina bit her lip. "Look, I know I won't be here much longer, but I could print out the paperwork for you and give you some advice tonight. It's well worth doing. And it'll draw a lot of people to your guesthouse when it opens."

"I don't want to get the word out too soon. It's going to take a long time to finish, with the hours Buck and I work."

"Hey, hey," said a man sitting across from Amy. "Don't blame me. Buck has worked so much overtime that he could do half days for the rest of the year and be okay." He looked at Gina. "I'm his so-called boss, Troy Hinton," he said, reaching out to shake her hand.

"Yeah, but I can't take time off, and the work we need to do now, like hanging wallpaper, requires two people," Lacey said. "I'm working extra hours myself, just to try to raise enough money so I can quit my day job and focus on the guesthouse when it opens. *If* it ever opens."

"I've hung tons of wallpaper." For Bobby's sake, Gina forced herself to persist. "I could just stay a little while and help—"

"No!" Lacey's voice cracked, causing conversation around the table to pause momentarily. "Not happening."

Gina felt her face heating with embarrassment.

Buck leaned toward his sister and spoke to her rapidly, and Lacey's eyes filled with tears.

One of the people who'd just come to the table, a pretty Asian American–looking woman who'd been introduced as Susan, shoved her plate away and came around the table to Lacey's side just as Lacey stood and murmured a broken apology to Gina.

"Come on," Susan said. "I'll take you home."

"Sorry about that," Buck said to Gina after Lacey and Susan were gone and conversation had resumed. "She has issues related to some stuff that's happened to her. She miscarried a baby, and quite honestly, I don't know if she'll ever recover. Lacey's strong in some ways, but she takes things hard."

"Oh, no! How awful!" Being a mother was the best thing that had ever happened to

Gina, and she could only imagine how losing a baby would feel. "I'm so sorry I upset her."

"Not your fault."

It wasn't, but how sad. Gina sighed and distracted herself by looking around the room at the tables full of people eating and talking. Up by the stage, a group of kids tossed around a couple of sponge balls, their laughter and shouts contributing to the general noise. Near the pass-through to the kitchen, women were cutting and serving pie, and the scents of cinnamon and nutmeg made Gina's mouth water. It smelled like the home of the girl she'd most envied back in her grade-school days, a girl who'd come from a big, warm family.

Behind her, she heard the sound of a baby crying, and she stood and turned at the same moment as the man who'd spoken about Buck being able to take time off. In the doorway of the fellowship hall, one of the nursery workers scanned the room, holding a crying Bobby. When she saw Gina, she waved, indicating that she'd bring Bobby over.

"Oh, yours, not ours," Troy said, sitting back down.

"Woot!" The woman next to him gave him a gentle high five. "We actually get to finish our meals. I'm Angelica, by the way," she said to Gina.

"Yeah, until Xavier gets too wild and we have to rein him in." Troy put an arm around Angelica, looking at her with warm possessiveness. "I have to fight for adult time with my wife."

The loving look she gave him back made jealousy knife through Gina's heart. Would she ever have a relationship like that, or was she doomed to repeat past failures?

Shaking off the jealousy, Gina thanked the nursery worker and pulled Bobby into her lap, cuddling him close. He was what was important, not her own romantic longings.

"He's adorable!" Angelica said. "How old is he?"

"Ten months." Gina nuzzled Bobby's head and wiped his tears.

"He's a big boy!" Angelica leaned forward to tickle Bobby's arm, making him chortle. "My Emmie is nine months, but she's nowhere near this one's size."

"Mom!" A boy of seven or eight hurtled into Angelica's side and then looked curiously at Bobby. "Who's that baby?"

Another little girl, a year or two younger, hopped into Angelica's lap. "Xavier took my dancing bear, Aunt Angelica."

"I just hid it, Mindy. It's behind the curtain." Xavier gestured toward the stage and leaned forward to tickle Bobby's knee.

Mindy stuck out her tongue at him, slid off Angelica's lap and ran toward the stage. At which point Gina realized that the little girl was missing a hand.

"Be kind to your cousin," Angelica scolded her son gently. "Go play with her."

"But she wants to play dumb games."

"Listen to your mother," Troy said, his

voice stern, and Xavier stuck out his lower lip, then nodded and ran toward Mindy.

As people watched and chuckled and asked to hold Bobby, Gina felt a sense of homecoming unlike anything she'd ever experienced before. She loved it here. She wanted to raise Bobby here.

An elderly woman approached their table, pushing a rolling walker. "Are you going to finish putting my house back together before the festival?" she asked, pointing a bony finger at Buck.

"Um, I don't think so, Miss Minnie."

"Why not?"

"Too much to do and not enough time to do it, with Lacey and me both working."

Amy explained. "The guesthouse belonged to Miss Minnie until recently."

"Was it in your family a long time?" Gina pushed her mostly empty plate aside, too interested to finish her meal.

"Since before the Civil War," the woman

said. "And to think that I would be the one to let it go out of the family…"

"Do you have any records, letters, stories?" Gina asked, fascinated as always by living local history.

"I certainly do, young lady. A whole trunk full of them. And you are…?"

"I'm sorry." Gina stood. "Would you like to sit down? I'm Gina Patterson. I'm…" She glanced around. "I'm just passing through, I guess. But I used to volunteer at the historical society where I lived in California. I hope those documents will be able to stay with the house."

"First time anyone's shown any interest," Miss Minnie grumbled.

"Sit down and join us, Miss Minnie," Buck said, standing too and holding a chair for the woman.

"No, sirree. I have more people to visit." And she was off, pushing her walker with surprising speed.

"Sure would be great if Lacey could open

the house in time for the festival," someone said.

Let me help. Gina had to press her lips together to keep from saying the words out
loud. "What kind of guests come to town
during the festival?" she asked instead.

"Last year, we got over three thousand
visitors." Troy had his arm around Angelica, unconsciously stroking her hair as he
spoke. "City people, mostly, from Cleveland
and Pittsburgh and Columbus. People who
like the small-town scene."

"People with money?" Amy asked.

A pretty, plump blonde woman lifted an
eyebrow at Amy. "You planning to pick
pockets?"

"Daisy!" Angelica shook her head. "Be
nice to Amy. She's newly back in town."

"And no," Amy said, laughing, "I'm not
picking anyone's pocket. I'm hoping to take
the visitors' money, but honestly. If I stay, I
might open up a shop."

Gina opened her mouth and then shut it again.

"What?" Angelica asked, and Buck looked curious, too.

"It's just...you couldn't *pay* for the kind of advertising Lacey would get if she could have an open house during the festival. Even if it was just partially done, a few rooms. The people who come to town are already looking for the small-town experience. They're perfect customers."

"For sure," Buck said. "Just don't see how we could get it done in time."

Angelica looked at Gina. "Could you help them? Because this might be a God thing."

"I... Yeah, I could."

"How?" Buck asked sharply.

"It's not just the historical-society work and the fact that I've done a lot of decorating. I also majored in marketing in college."

"So you know how to showcase a place like the guesthouse to make it shine, right?" Angelica asked, smiling as if she already knew the answer.

"Yeah," Gina admitted, "I do. The place would be booked for months in advance even before it officially opens. Especially if there aren't a lot of competing guesthouses and B and Bs here."

"There's just the one other motel," Buck said, "and it's very basic." He looked thoughtful, as if he were really considering the possibility of having Gina stay and help.

"You and Lacey should totally hire her," Angelica said.

"Well, but it would mean having Bobby around a lot." Now that Buck seemed to be considering the idea, all the reasons against it flooded into Gina's head. "And we'd have to stay there. If we could stay, your sister could pay me pretty minimally."

"I can take Bobby some," Angelica said unexpectedly. "I'm at home with Emmie, and it would be fun for her to have a playmate."

"I couldn't pay much for child care," Gina

warned, feeling uncomfortable with the need to economize. But she was determined to learn—or relearn—to live without the easy wealth she'd gotten accustomed to during her marriage.

Angelica waved a hand. "You wouldn't need to pay. It could be our contribution to the guesthouse. Rescue River needs it badly."

"No, I'd find a way to pay. But that would be great. There are fumes in some parts of a renovation, and that wouldn't be good for him. Would it, sweetie?" She reached out her arms for Bobby, who was snuggling now in Buck's arms.

"I'll hold him—it's fine," he said. "All of this is a good idea for Rescue River and for Lacey. But I have my doubts about whether…" He broke off, looked down at Bobby and then back at Gina, his face bleak. "Like I said, having a baby around would be hard on her."

And on you, Gina thought.

Around them, clattering dishes and bustling footsteps announced that the meal was coming to an end, but at their table, everyone was watching Buck.

Abruptly, he handed Bobby back to Gina and lifted his hands like stop signs. "All right, all right. I'll talk to her again. But I can't make any promises. I doubt she'll agree to anything of the kind."

As for Gina, she wondered whether Buck would present a fair case. He seemed almost as set against her staying as his sister was.

On Monday and Tuesday, Buck busied himself with work at the vet clinic. His boss, Troy Hinton, took in every animal who had a need, whether the owners could pay or not, so there was plenty of work.

Midafternoon on Tuesday, Buck was washing up after a procedure when there was a sharp click and then someone crowded behind him.

Adrenaline surged. Buck spun, wet hands up, and grabbed for his assailant's throat.

"Hey, hey!" His boss's surprised voice and familiar face made Buck drop his hands and step back, heart racing.

He looked away and drew in a couple of deep breaths, like they'd taught him at the VA.

"You okay?" Troy's voice was mild as he put away a pair of surgical forceps and started washing his hands at the other side of the sink.

"Yeah. Sorry, man."

"I should know better than to sneak up behind you." Troy dried off and then sat down at the computer.

It was a great thing about working for Troy Hinton: he was calm, an old friend, and he'd known about Buck's PTSD—and his other flaws—when he'd hired him.

His heart still racing, Buck stepped out the back door of the clinic for some air…and heard a whining, scratching sound at his feet.

There was a closed cardboard box, a couple of feet square, with holes punched in the sides and an envelope on the top. Uh-oh.

He picked up the box and carried it inside. "Drop-off," he said to Troy and set the box down on the floor. He handed the envelope to Troy, then grabbed a pair of forceps and used them to open the box gingerly. No telling what he might find. Could be something wild and scared, even rabid.

But when he got the box open, a dirty white mop flung itself out and planted front paws on Buck's leg. When he bent to pat what looked like its head, the little dog licked his hand, barking and whining.

He squatted down. "Okay, buddy. It's okay." He stroked the matted, dirty fur. "What's in the envelope?" he asked Troy.

Troy squinted at a sheet of notepaper and then read aloud. "'I'm sick, can't take care of Spike no more. My kids want to put him down. Please help.'"

"Spike?" Buck brushed back the excessive

hair on the little dog's head and looked into anxious dark eyes. "You're a tough guy, huh?"

A couple of bills fluttered to the floor, and Troy picked them up, a five and a single. "Six dollars." He shook his head. "Guy probably went without something to leave that."

"Got room for him at the rescue?"

"I'll make room. Better check him out first." Troy got a small biscuit out of the jar they kept on the desk and whistled, and the mop waddled over to him. "Hey, big guy. How long were you out there?"

The little dog's whole body wagged.

"Sit," Troy said, and the mop sat down and held out a polite paw. When Troy offered the biscuit, the dog grabbed it and ran off to the corner of the room to eat. "He's hungry."

"Somebody trained him, though. Can't figure why anyone would want to put the little guy down." Buck stood. "Want me to do an exam?"

"No. I want you to take afternoons off like you're supposed to and go work on your sister's guesthouse. Why are you even here, come to think of it?"

Buck shrugged. "I meant to, but…"

"But what? What's going on?"

Buck blew out a sigh. He'd told himself he was needed here, but the truth was more complicated.

"Avoiding Gina and Bobby?" Troy sat down in the rolling chair and crossed his arms.

"Might be." Of course he was. He'd convinced his sister to give the new situation with Gina a try, and now he wasn't sure it had been the right thing.

"How come? You gotta deal with stuff, man, not let it slip under the rug."

And this was the bad thing about working for Troy: he was a little too insightful. "She's kicking up some memories, and not just for Lacey."

"Go home," Troy ordered.

"You're sure—"

"I'm sure."

* * *

So that was how, the next morning, Buck found himself just outside a smallish bedroom, listening to Bobby's baby chatter and Gina's murmurs.

He was almost wishing he hadn't talked Lacey into allowing Gina to stay and help. "Until the Freedom Festival and not a moment longer," Lacey had said.

Even that amount of time might be too long.

He, Lacey and Gina had talked last night, figuring out a plan. Lacey would open half of the house for the Freedom Festival, so people could see the progress and get excited about coming to stay, and then work on the rest of the house throughout the summer and possibly into the fall.

And right now, his role was to work afternoons—and possibly evenings—with Gina to finish the three rooms. Mornings, when he was working at the clinic, she'd be figuring out the historical-landmark paperwork and setting up a website to publicize the guesthouse.

Bobby was on hands and knees next to a table Gina had set up in the middle of the room. As Buck watched, the sturdy baby grabbed the leg of the table, hauled himself to his feet and then fell right back down on his diaper-clad behind. Undaunted, he reached for the table leg and began to repeat the process.

Gina bent over a book that lay open on the table. She tucked a lock of hair behind her ear and looked from the book to a can of something—paint, maybe—and then back at the book again.

Man, she's pretty. Buck's heart kicked up to a faster rate. Ignoring that, he tapped on the door frame.

"Hey." Gina smiled when she saw him, eyes sparkling, and his heart rate jumped up another notch. "I thought we'd start with the simplest project," she said. "Come see what I... I mean, we...have planned."

Calm down, buddy—she's not for you. He walked into the room, deliberately not focusing on Gina.

It was a corner bedroom with windows on two sides, and Gina had opened them. Birds chittered madly outside and a fresh breeze cooled his face.

"It's a little chilly in here, but I figure we'll get warm as we work. I like having the windows open, because we're going to be using primer today and I don't like him breathing it." She looked down at Bobby, her face curving into a smile, and Buck realized that the baby had pulled himself up again and stood, banging on the table leg, grinning.

"The fresh air is no problem. If you want to work on filling nail holes and doing repairs, I can do the priming in a different room from where you and Bobby are."

"I've already done that. And I cleaned the walls. So now, it's down to whether you prefer doing the edges with a brush or rolling." She held up a paintbrush and roller.

"Rolling is more fun for sure, but let's both work on the edges a little. That takes twice as long."

"Great."

While Buck opened two cans of primer and stirred them up, Gina brought out a pack-and-play. She put Bobby inside, along with a stack of plastic blocks and vinyl-covered books. "That'll keep him for a while, and when he gets bored, maybe he'll take a little nap." Gina bit her lip, her forehead wrinkling.

"You're short of toys for him."

She shrugged. "He's used to having a lot more stuff to entertain him, but it's okay. It'll develop his imagination."

"I know where you can get a bunch of baby stuff, free." He hadn't known he was going to offer until it happened, and the moment the words were out of his mouth, he regretted it.

Her forehead smoothed out. "I would love it, if you're serious. It's a challenge to entertain an active baby in the workplace."

"You've been doing fine." Maybe she'd decide she didn't want the loan.

"I'm fortunate that Susan Hayashi brought over the pack-and-play and a few toys. Apparently, they belonged to her fiancé and were just stored in his basement."

"I'm sure Sam Hinton had nothing but the best for Mindy. He's a pretty wealthy guy." But Buck didn't envy the CEO of Hinton Enterprises for his millions. The man had lost his wife and had struggled for a couple of years to deal with issues related to his daughter's disability and reaction to losing her mother. He'd only recently started looking happy and energetic again, since Susan Hayashi had come into his life last summer.

"So, where's this cache of baby toys?" she asked as she turned on the radio. "Is it your old stuff? GI Joes?"

"No...though I did have my share of those, and don't you dare call them dolls." He was hoping to distract her, and it worked.

"You grew up here in Rescue River, right? What did your parents do?"

Buck dipped his brush and started to paint a careful edge, finding the meticulous work soothing. "Yeah. Dad sold cars and Mom…" He paused, thinking how to explain it. "Mom taught piano when she could."

"Sounds like a story." Gina knelt to apply primer around a window frame.

"Yeah." Buck let out a mirthless chuckle. "It's a real old story. When Lacey and I were little, she just had a couple of cocktails before dinner. By the time we were teenagers, it was pills to get going in the morning and wine with lunch."

"Oh, I'm sorry." Gina glanced his way, compassion in her eyes, and shook her head. "That's so hard to deal with."

"Your husband had similar issues, right?"

She nodded, but didn't bite at the change of subject. "Is your mom still living?"

"No. Died when I was twenty-one." He was so used to saying it that he felt just a twinge of sadness, nothing more. Mom had been too talented for a small town, and too East Coast for Ohio, and actually, she'd been absent to him and Lacey for several years before her death.

The quick squeeze of his shoulder surprised him. "I'm sorry for your loss. And for having to grow up that way."

Quickly, Buck shook his head. "It wasn't like that. Lacey and I were blessed. Dad's a great guy. Everyone in town loved him. And his parents—my gram and gramps—they filled in the gaps when Mom wasn't doing well. It was hard on Lacey, not having a mom who could help her with the girl things. But for me, it was a real good childhood."

"So how come you started drinking?"

Just like that, Buck's easy mood shattered into pieces. Bobby was standing in the pack-and-play, waving his arms, and Buck put down his brush and went over to pick the boy up, craving the comfort. "Drank a little during the war. And a lot after. It would've taken a better man than I am to do two tours in Afghanistan without drinking."

She nodded, moving over to the next window frame and running the paintbrush along it with easy skill.

The fact that she wasn't looking at him, and the comfortable feel of Bobby in his arms, made him go on. "Got worse when I lost my wife and child. They say there's a genetic factor with alcoholism, and it looks like I inherited it." Gently, he set Bobby down in the playpen and, when the boy started to fuss, located his binky and popped it into his mouth. Then he pulled out the stepladder that had been lying along one wall and set it up. "What about you? Did you grow up in California?"

"Yes. Sacramento."

"What do your parents do?" He wondered why she hadn't gone to them when she'd had the trouble with her in-laws.

"I never knew my mom," she said. "And Dad...well, he's got his own life. He's homesteading in Alaska with a group of friends. Kind of a back-to-nature thing."

She said it carelessly, similar to the way Buck talked about his own mother. "I didn't think homesteading even existed anymore."

"It doesn't, not the way it used to be, land for work. They're subsistence farming on public land. No electricity, no cell phones… It's pretty basic."

"Does he know you're in trouble? Can he help you?"

Gina just shook her head a little, a smile curving her lips. "Dad's not the type to rush in and save his daughter. He's a dreamer, always broke. I'm actually just glad he's got these friends to stay with. That way, I don't have to worry about him."

Interesting. Gina was in a tight spot herself, but she talked about her father like the man was another child, not someone she could turn to. "Have you been up there to visit?" He was wondering if it would be a viable place for Gina to go and stay with Bobby for a while. She seemed to want to hide.

The thought of her leaving Rescue River, though, put a very alarming pressure on his heart.

"I surprised him on his fiftieth birthday. Took a bunch of books and supplies. It was kind of fun."

"What was it like?" For whatever reason, he wanted to keep her talking. Her voice was low for a woman, a little husky, and the sound of it sent a pleasant sensation rippling down his spine.

"Well, fishing for our dinner was an adventure. And hauling water really is good exercise." She flexed her arm, making a muscle, and tossed a saucy grin his way.

The air whooshed out of his lungs. She was, quite literally, breathtaking when she smiled that funny, relaxed smile.

"But there was a downside." She wrinkled her nose. "I really prefer indoor plumbing, especially when it's cold outside."

"I can imagine. And it doesn't sound like a good place for a baby."

"No. I never even considered it." Gina stretched her back and shoulders, flipped her ponytail and returned to work.

Which Buck needed to do, too. He didn't need to think about how lively and pretty Gina was, how her attitude toward what sounded like a pretty neglectful dad wasn't bitter. How she saw the humor in a situation that some would have resented.

Bobby had been pulling himself up at the edge of the pack-and-play, and now he started to climb. He fell back and immediately tried again.

"It's just a matter of time until he figures out how to escape," Gina said, watching him. "If you were serious about finding him some other toys, sooner might be better than later."

"Um, sure." *Be a man*, he told himself. But dread filled his heart.

Chapter Six

Buck really, really didn't want to do this.

And if he had to visit the place he'd avoided for a year and a half, he didn't want an audience. "Are you sure you want to come along? I can do it myself," he offered again as his stomach knotted tight.

"No, it's fine. I'd like to come. I know what kind of stuff Bobby likes, and if he has an outing now, he'll settle down better later on. We haven't gotten out much since I sent away my SUV." She was fastening Bobby into his car seat as she talked. Then she climbed into the passenger seat of the truck.

Which left Buck no choice but to get in and

drive. He turned on the radio so he wouldn't have to talk.

All too soon, they approached the little cottage, set back from the road with a big grassy yard, a garden on one side. He looked away from the house and the memories.

Tightening his jaw, he drove down the rutted driveway to the garage, took his time about turning the truck around so it would be easy to load things into the back.

Then he couldn't postpone getting out any longer, so he cut the engine and opened the door.

The sound of the rushing creek and chirping birds filled his ears, and the smell of earth rose up to him. He couldn't help but glance at the garden, notice it was turned over. The tenant must be eager to get to gardening.

Like Ivana had always been.

"Who lives here?" Gina asked as she freed Bobby from his car seat and set him down, holding his hands so he could toddle. "See the bird?" she asked, kneeling and pointing to a robin that was hopping through the shining green grass.

"A single mom," he said noncommittally. "Couple of kids, I think."

"Don't you have to talk to her first?"

He paused, hand on the garage door handle. "It's my place. She rents the house, but not the garage."

He didn't look at her, but he heard her soft "oh."

The sooner he raised the garage door, the sooner he could get done and get out of here. "It's a mess," he warned and slid the door open.

He stared at the ground for a minute, not wanting to look. Not wanting to kick up the memories of the day when he'd cleaned out their house, alone, in a drunk frenzy of pain. He felt ashamed, now, of how he'd thrown everything in here. He'd probably broken some stuff that would have been perfectly useful to someone in need.

"It's actually kind of neat." Gina walked past him to stand in the doorway of the garage, squinting to see, and he looked up and realized she was right. Toys were stacked along one wall, alongside some labeled boxes. Furniture and more boxes lined the rest of the garage.

There was a sound behind them, and they both turned. A pretty redhead stood there with a couple of kids behind her, one probably first grade, the other littler, maybe three. "Hi, I'm Cassie. And you must be Buck Armstrong? I hope you don't mind. Your sister and I straightened everything out a couple of months after I moved in. We were afraid it was a fire hazard."

"It's fine." He introduced himself and Gina, welcoming the distraction. Then Gina introduced Bobby and showed him to the little kids, doing that instant bonding thing women—especially women with kids—were so good at doing.

Ivana hadn't been that good at it, and she'd

complained about feeling left out at the playground and swimming pool. It was part of the reason they'd chosen to live out here: she'd been more of a loner.

"Would you like me to take Bobby into the backyard for a little bit, so you can focus?" Cassie asked. "It's fenced in and we have some fun climbing toys."

"Um…" Gina hesitated, obviously reluctant to leave Bobby with a stranger. "I wouldn't want to inconvenience you."

"Just bring him over if you'd like." Cassie started walking back toward the play area in the backyard, surrounded by a white picket fence.

He'd put in that fence himself, so Mia could play safely as she grew.

He clenched a fist and forced that thought away. "She's safe. A nice lady. Lacey checked her references."

"It would be so good for Bobby to be able to climb and play with her kids. And I can watch him from here… Okay. I'll be right back."

Grimly, Buck strode into the garage and pulled out the two biggest boxes labeled Toys. He was going back in for more when Gina returned. "Go ahead and look through the boxes," he said as he pulled out a high chair. Mia's high chair. He put it down and turned to Gina. "Take whatever you think he'd like. We should do this quick."

She glanced up at him speculatively. "Look, I didn't realize… I totally understand if—"

"It's fine." It had been almost three years. He could deal with this. To prove it, he knelt beside the nearest box and started pulling stuff out randomly.

There were some toys he didn't even remember, a shape-sorter thing full of triangles and squares, a little phone, some dolls. Stuff that looked new. Gifts, probably, meant for when Mia got older.

Gina pulled an empty box out of the truck and sat down beside him on the grass. She started inspecting the toys he'd gotten out, murmuring almost to herself. "This one's got some little parts—better not take that. But he'd love that light-up ball. He doesn't play with dolls, not yet, but I think it's fine for boys to play with dolls. Maybe if there's a boy one..."

Her words soothed him. He was doing fine. He was handling this.

He pulled out a bucket and shovel, and an image of the week they'd spent at the beach came back to him. Sitting with Mia in the sand, showing her how to dig, watching her giggle as the water touched her toes. Ivana hurrying over with an umbrella, scolding him, but mildly. They'd gotten along great that week.

"Go ahead and take anything." He got up quickly and walked back into the dark garage.

He found the ExerSaucer he'd had in mind when he'd first proposed this harebrained idea. Beside it was a little seat on cables, and he remembered that it was a door jumper

Mia had loved. He swallowed and grabbed that, too.

As he came out of the garage into the sunlight, Gina looked his way and her eyes lit up. "Oh, wow, that'd be so great if we could borrow the ExerSaucer!"

This was worth it, to see that happiness in her eyes, to find a way to lighten her burden.

And then he saw what she had in her hand.

Mia's pink elephant. Her lovey. The toy she'd slept with every night and nap time. She'd just started insisting that they take it everywhere, a new phase, when she and Ivana had disappeared that last, fateful time. When he'd seen it lying on the couch, he'd figured they'd be right back, had stopped worrying about them.

Mia hadn't even had her lovey in those scary, horrible final moments.

Without realizing he'd moved, he had the elephant in his hands. He turned it over to look at the toe she'd always sucked on. Held the slightly dirty-looking creature to his face.

When he smelled it—smelled *Mia*—everything he'd been trying to forget came rushing back.

He could feel her in his arms, could hear her cry. He remembered what it had been like to walk the floor with her, bouncing her gently, helping her calm down. Feeding her a bottle. Tickling her into a good mood.

Putting her down in her crib for a nap. And when she'd reach up her arms to him, wanting to be held when she really needed sleep, he'd put Pinky into her arms and she would sigh and cuddle her elephant.

Somehow, he found his way over to the side of the garage where he could be alone. He squatted down, his back against the wall, drawing his arms and legs in while physical pain racked his chest. His throat and eyes felt swollen and he could barely breathe.

He let his head drop to his chest, held the little pink elephant to his face and fell apart.

* * *

Gina steered the truck into its parking space at the guesthouse and looked over at Buck.

He was staring straight ahead, his whole body rigid.

Guilt washed over her at having been the catalyst for all this pain. She'd known plenty of grief herself, losing her husband, but the loss of a child was unimaginable. She opened the door and extracted Bobby from his car seat, held him close and looked at Buck.

Who could never hold his baby close again. She swallowed hard. "Do you want to…? Can I do anything for you? Call someone? Do you want to talk?" She was babbling, asking too many questions, but it seemed better than letting him deal with all of this alone.

She'd seen men cry before. Her dad had wiped tears when he'd learned that his sister had passed away. And her father-in-law had gotten a little choked up at Hank's funeral.

But to see this big, tough veteran truly break down… Whoa. That was a first. Even after she'd given him some privacy, had loaded the truck and gotten Bobby into his car seat, the sight of Buck hunched there, shoulders still shaking a little, had made her cry, too. She'd had to grab a handful of tissues and pull herself together before she could help him to his feet and drive him home. Because this wasn't about her; it was about him.

"No. I'm… Let's get this stuff unloaded. Got to do a couple errands." He opened the car door and got out, moving mechanically to the back of the truck.

"You don't have to…"

"I got this." He lifted the box and the couple of big toys out and carried them up to the house.

Unsure how to help, she followed him, carrying Bobby.

He had the things in her room before she'd gotten halfway up the stairs. "Can I have the keys?" he asked, his voice expressionless.

And then he took them from her and drove off for parts unknown.

A couple of hours later, when he came back, Gina deliberately gave him his space, staying in her room with a book she'd checked out from the Rescue River library. But when Bobby woke up hungry, and she heard voices downstairs, she decided she had to come out of her room.

Shifting Bobby on her hip—man, was he getting heavy!—Gina walked down the curving wooden staircase and into the large, old-fashioned kitchen.

Buck, pouring coffee at the counter, didn't turn around. But at the table, three curious faces turned her way, and two older gentlemen stood. "You sit down right here, sweetheart," said the one with an impeccable comb-over, a dress shirt and expensive-looking slacks and shoes.

"Don't be ridiculous, Hinton. My seat is closer." The other man, shorter and stocky, dressed in a flannel shirt and work pants, held the chair he'd been sitting in, at the end of the table.

Feeling like she was walking into something she didn't quite understand, Gina sat in the closest chair and set Bobby down beside her. "Thank you both. I'm Gina Patterson, and this is my son, Bobby."

"Pleased to meet you," said the slender, gray-haired woman at the table, holding out a hand to grasp Gina's. "I'm Lou Ann Miller, and this is Elias Hinton and Roscoe Camden. And you two men can sit down. Honestly! There are plenty of chairs."

Buck brought over cups of coffee, a sugar bowl and a creamer, waving off Lou Ann's offer of help. "You sit," he said. "The water's almost boiling for tea, if you'd rather have that."

Lou Ann held out for tea while Gina and the men accepted coffee.

"What brings you to Rescue River?" Mr. Camden asked bluntly. "We've been hearing different stories at the Senior Towers."

"Leave the woman alone," Mr. Hinton ordered. "You shouldn't listen to all of the tall tales over there."

"That place *is* a hotbed of gossip," Lou Ann said. "There's no need for you to fill us in on your personal business, dear."

"Thanks." Gina smiled apologetically at Mr. Camden. "It *is* somewhat personal, but I'm hoping to stay awhile. It's a lovely town."

"Quite a history, too," Mr. Hinton said. Bobby was holding on to the leg of his chair, looking up with curiosity, and Mr. Hinton reached down and picked him up, handing him a teaspoon to bang on the table.

"The house's history is just what I'm interested in." Gina seized on the topic. "I'm helping Lacey apply to put this house on the National Register of Historic Places, and I'd like to learn more about the background of the house and the area. Do you all have any ideas where I could find out more?"

Buck chuckled as he sat down at the table, pushing a teacup toward Lou Ann and dunking his own tea bag. "You've just opened a big can of worms. These three know everything about the town. From three very distinct viewpoints."

Fifteen minutes and a rousing argument later, Gina had appointments to meet with all three of them, and the elders made their departure.

When Buck came back into the kitchen, Gina raised an eyebrow at him as she gathered up the coffee cups. "Why do I feel like I've been through a war?"

"Longest-lasting love triangle in Rescue River."

Buck looked at Bobby, who was chanting, "Up! Up!" He reached down and swept the baby into his arms.

A tingle of awareness passed through Gina's chest at the sight of her son against the rugged veteran's broad chest. A few teaspoons slipped out of her hands and clattered on the floor.

Instantly Buck was across the room, sliding Bobby to his hip and kneeling gracefully, helping her to pick them up.

The tingle intensified.

It wasn't just his physical grace or his good manners. It was what she'd learned about him this afternoon. Somehow, the fact that he had the capacity for that much emotion had made Buck twice as appealing to her.

Gina ducked her heated face away from him and deposited the spoons in the sink. "Thanks. Clumsy of me."

He rose lightly, his white teeth flashing in a smile. "That's not the word I'd think of to describe you."

Their gazes held for a beat too long.

"Listen," Gina said, "I'm sorry to have opened up old wounds earlier today. Are you okay?"

He nodded. "Embarrassed. You think you're over something and then it hits you."

"That's grief," she agreed. "Don't be embarrassed. It's natural."

"I guess." He blew out a breath. "I don't mean to be rude, but could we drop the subject?"

"Oh, sure! I'm sorry."

He touched her chin. "Don't take it personally. At all. I needed to do that, I guess, but now... I feel like I've been hit by a truck. I can't handle getting run over again today."

"Makes sense." Gina tore her gaze away and rinsed dishes while Buck carried the rest of the dishes to the sink, still holding Bobby. "I guess I'll have to take a little time off from wallpapering to talk with the folks who were just here, but I hope that won't be a problem. I know you have to spend some time at the clinic, too. And we don't always have to be working together. There's some stuff I can do alone, or you can. A lot of stuff, actually." *Stop babbling, stop babbling.*

While she felt flustered, Buck seemed perfectly composed. "Time away from the house isn't a problem. We're not punching time cards here, just trying to get the work done."

"Hey, Gina." Lacey's voice, behind them, provided a welcome respite from her worries. "I came home for..." She saw Buck holding

Bobby and swallowed visibly. "For an early dinner," she said, her voice quiet.

Gina's heart ached. She and Bobby didn't mean to, but they kept causing pain. "Sit down and I'll fix you something. Fix all of us something. We may as well eat before we go back to work," she added to Buck.

"No. Hey, I think I'll just head on back. I don't have much time." Now Lacey's voice sounded choked. Her cat, Mr. Whiskers, meowed loudly, and she picked him up and held him close to her chest. "Hey, buddy, where's your wife, huh? Where's Mrs. Whiskers?"

Gina shot Buck a glance, the same one he was sending to her. Again, that something arced between them. She took Bobby out of his arms, opened the fridge and grabbed a bowl of mashed potatoes and peas from last night's dinner. "On second thought, I think I'll feed Bobby first," she said as she headed for the porch.

She'd give Buck a chance to talk to his sister, give Lacey some space in her own house.

And meanwhile, she'd remind herself not to pay attention to the occasional sparks between herself and Buck. She needed to remember she had bad judgment with men. Just look at the mistake she'd made in her marriage.

Anyway, Buck had mentioned leaving Rescue River. He seemed to fit here, but he'd said he was moving on soon.

She looked down the street toward the library and restaurant that marked the beginning of the town's small business district. It was unusually warm for this time of year, and despite its being a weekday, lots of people were out. She saw two mothers walking along with babies in strollers. A small group of older people clustered on the benches in front of the Senior Towers. And a group of teenagers stood talking in front of the library, their excited voices floating to her on the warm breeze.

This was where she wanted to raise Bobby, God willing. She wanted to take him to the library and show him off to the seniors. To shop at the little market.

And this was where Buck *didn't* want to be. Another reason not to get involved.

Through the screen door, she heard Buck's rumbling voice and Lacey's quiet one. Good. That was what Lacey needed, to talk to her brother.

That, and not to have a baby in her face every moment.

Gina breathed in the smell of the earth, thawing in the weak sunshine of early March. A few daffodils were pushing up beside the porch steps, and she set Bobby's food down and carried him into the yard to let him crawl in the grass. She wished she'd thought to put a jacket on him, but she'd been rushing to escape.

She needed to do something different about Bobby if she was going to stay here and help with the renovations. His presence was causing Lacey pain, and while it was inevitable that he should be around Lacey sometimes, the woman ought to be able to come home for a peaceful dinner without getting her wounds, whatever they were, ripped open.

Bobby had crawled over to the fence, and as she watched, he pulled himself up to stare out between the slats. It wasn't good for him to be trapped in the house with paint and renovation tools and overbusy adults. The new toys were great, but he needed more stimulation, more attention.

She pulled her phone out of her back pocket and found Angelica's number. She was just finalizing the arrangements to have her care for Bobby three days per week when Buck came out onto the porch.

When she ended the call, Buck lifted an eyebrow. "You're taking Bobby somewhere?"

"To Angelica's," she tossed over her shoulder, jogging to get the baby before he figured out that the front gate was open. She swept him up and blew on his belly, causing him to chortle gleefully. Then she hugged him close and climbed back up the porch steps. "He's going to stay with her three days per week. That way, I can focus better on work."

"And Lacey won't see him as much." He gave her a half smile. "Thanks for that."

She nodded, holding Bobby, as the March sun tried to warm her back. His eyes warmed her more and she drew in a quick breath, unable to look away.

But all at once his face seemed to close and he turned. And that was good, she told herself firmly. She busied herself settling Bobby on her lap and spooning potatoes into his mouth, getting a little inside him before letting him try with the spoon, which would lead to a mess.

Best to remember that Buck had his secrets, his reasons to keep a distance. As did she. A little front-porch attraction didn't add up to anything in the lives of two people whose pasts were all too complicated.

Chapter Seven

Two days later, Buck held the door so that Gina could walk ahead of him into Love's Hardware. He tried not to notice the fruity smell of her shampoo.

They'd dropped Bobby off at Angelica's and now were picking up some supplies before another day of renovation.

He was spending too much time with her. The pink of her cheeks, the light smattering of freckles across her nose, the gentle sway of her walk—all of it held far too much of his attention.

"Wow." Gina stood staring at the crowded array of garbage cans, lamp oil, electrical cords, gutter spouts, hammers and pipes. "It's truly everything but the kitchen sink."

"We have those, too," said a voice above them. "Back left corner of the store."

At the sound, both Buck and Gina looked up.

As Buck had suspected, the voice came from Harold Love, the wiry, white-haired African American store owner, who stood at the top of a tall stepladder. He was sliding a large box from the high shelf above the store's sales racks.

"Hey, Mr. Love, it's Buck Armstrong," he called, knowing the old man's vision wasn't the best.

"I was just praying for a little help here. Buck, son, if I drop this down, can you catch it for me?"

"But that's huge—" Gina's eyes widened.

"Right here." Buck stepped forward, feeling an absurd desire to impress her with his strength.

Mr. Love dropped the box, and Buck caught

it easily. It was light, probably containing some type of paper product.

Gina touched his arm and nodded over at Mr. Love, who was now climbing down the ladder, slow but steady. "Is he okay?" she whispered.

Buck set the box down on the floor and nodded. "Don't worry about Mr. Love. He's been doing this for more than fifty years." All the same, he took a step closer, ready to help the man if needed.

"Grandpa!" A pretty, heavyset young woman came bustling from the back of the store. "Did you climb up there yourself after I told you not to?" She turned to Buck and Gina. "His vision is getting worse. He's not supposed to do things like that."

"Now you just let me be, Aliyah." Mr. Love reached the floor unassisted and smiled in their general direction. "Thank you for the help, young man." He headed back toward the counter, using his hands to unobtrusively guide himself, moving confidently.

He seemed to have an inner picture of every item of stock and every inch of the store, so his visual impairment wasn't obvious to most people. He liked it that way, Buck knew.

Buck had renewed his old acquaintance with Mr. Love when he'd started working on Lacey's house, and he valued their friendship. It was all about nuts and bolts, paints and primers, plumbing and wiring. Unlike most of the other people in Rescue River, Mr. Love knew nothing of Buck's alcoholic antics, or at least, he hadn't been affected by them. The eightysomething man was a non-judgmental, easy part of Buck's past.

Aliyah scolded Mr. Love a little more before heading toward the back of the store, shaking her head.

Gina's phone pinged. She pulled it out, looked at it and frowned.

Curiosity tugged at him. Was she starting to make friends in town?

But whoever was texting her, it wasn't Buck's business. Deliberately, he focused on the familiar sights and sounds of the store. From hidden speakers, the sound of Smokey Robinson filled the air; it was all Motown, all the time here at Love's Hardware. A grinding sound in the back of the store told him a key was being made. The faint, acrid smell of lawn products permeated the very bones of the place.

Buck walked toward the counter, gesturing for Gina to follow along. "How's business today?" he asked the older man.

"Just fine, just fine, now that you've come in." Mr. Love patted his arm. "As soon as I heard it was you, I knew you wouldn't mind giving me a hand. Just like old times, eh, son?"

"That's right."

"Now, let me just carry this cleaning solution over to Miz Miriam's cart and I'll be right back to help you. Don't let anyone else take care of you. I want to help you myself. Aliyah and all the young folks want to put me out to pasture and I'm not having any of it." The old man hustled away, carrying the heavy jug of cleaning solution.

Buck saw Gina's raised eyebrows. "My first job when I was in high school. Mr. Love was a tough boss, but fair. He taught me a lot."

She smiled, and then her phone pinged again. Her face tightened, just briefly, but she didn't pull out her phone. Instead, she crossed her arms over her chest and looked around. "What an amazing place."

Mr. Love, returning to the cash-register area, heard her. "This hardware store has been in my family since 1901," he said proudly. "Now, what can I do for you people? Buck, son, you still working on Miss Minnie's old house?"

"That's right—trying to get some rooms open in time for the Freedom Festival."

"And we're looking to get it onto the National Register of Historic Places," Gina added. "If you've been in the area and familiar with the house for a long time, I might like to talk to you as I'm doing the paperwork."

"Have you talked to Miss Minnie yet?" Buck asked.

"We're supposed to meet soon. She's a busy lady."

"That she is." Mr. Love smiled. "I'd be honored to help. That house is a very important place to a lot of people in this town. *Very* important."

"How do you mean?" Gina asked. "If you have time to tell us about it."

Mr. Love perched on the high stool behind the counter. "Falcon Station was the stop before our place on the Underground Railroad."

"I knew the guesthouse was a stop," Gina said, "but I didn't know there were others nearby. Is yours still standing?"

"Standing, but not much more than that. The house is gone, but the old barn where travelers hid is still around, about ten miles up the road. Has a rose painted on the side that you can barely make out. Served to let folks know it was a safe place."

"I've seen it." Buck remembered driving by during some high-school carousing. A couple of older boys had warned him that any spray painting, egg throwing or sign shooting should steer clear of the Old Rose Barn. In turn, he'd passed along the message to younger boys when he was a senior.

"Could it be made into a national landmark, too, I wonder?"

Mr. Love beamed at Gina's interest. "I don't know about that. It's just one of those weathered, falling-down barns, though I've taken the kids and grandkids up there and told the story."

"Maybe we could see it sometime, too."

"You surely could," the older man said, "but the Falcon home has plenty to keep you busy exploring. Have you looked for the secret treasure in the cellar?"

"Treasure?"

"Or something hidden, anyway. Never saw it for myself, but that's the story."

Gina's eyes lit up again, and she gripped Buck's arm. "Have you explored the basement?"

"No way. It has a dirt floor and nasty cobwebs."

"Wimp," she said, scoffing at him. Her hand was still on his arm, her eyes full of fun. "Tell you what, soldier hero. I'll protect you if you'll go down there and explore it with me."

He lifted an eyebrow. "Will you hold my hand?"

"If you're good." Her lips quirked up at the corners.

Wow.

Her phone pinged again, and the smile faded from her face. She took it out, read the message, frowned and shoved it back in her purse, hard.

"Something wrong?" he asked as Mr. Love turned to assist another customer.

"Nothing. No big deal." She turned toward the rest of the store, straightening her shoulders, back to business. "Do you have a list?"

"It's all up here," he said, tapping the side of his head.

She rolled her eyes. "Great. Let's see how much you remember."

They headed to the drawer pulls and wall anchors they'd come for. Buck made his selections, and when he turned back toward Gina, she stood transfixed in front of a rack of gardening supplies, rakes and hoses and shovels. She was holding a packet of seeds in her hand.

He approached her. "You like gardening?" he asked.

"Just think what could be done with the little yard in front of the guesthouse."

He wasn't much for flowers, but he could imagine they'd look nice. The question was, if Gina planted flowers now, would she be around to see them blossom? Would he?

"I wonder why they called it Falcon Station?" she asked him.

"Miss Minnie's last name is Falcon." He lowered his voice. "Rumor has it that Mr. Love has been sweet on Miss Minnie for years."

She lifted an eyebrow. "The elders in this community are very…"

"Social? Romantic?" He grinned. "Something in the water, maybe."

Her phone pinged in her purse. And again. And again.

She squeezed her eyes shut for a moment, then pulled out her phone and looked at it. Her hand flew to her mouth.

"What's wrong?" Buck stepped closer, wanting to protect her from whatever was making her look so scared.

"They're cutting off my phone," she said faintly. "What am I going to do without a phone?"

"Who?"

"My in-laws. Bobby's grandparents." She

shook her head back and forth, her expression despairing. "What am I going to do? They're going to…" She trailed off and squeezed her eyes shut.

Buck's eyes narrowed. "They have some kind of control of your account?"

She pressed her lips together and then nodded. "I didn't think about it, but yes. I'm on their plan."

"Does your phone have a GPS?" he asked immediately.

She shook her head quickly. "I disabled that right away, as soon as I left. And I blocked them from being able to see my call log and turned off location services. I just… I guess I wasn't thinking about how they could cut off my phone. And it's not like I'm a phone addict or anything, but I need Angelica to be able to contact me about Bobby. I need that phone for emergencies."

"Ma'am?" Mr. Love's voice came from behind them. "We have some of those no-contract, prepaid cell phones."

She turned. "You do?"

"Right over here." He felt his way along the shelf to where a display stood. "Take your pick." He put a wrinkled hand on Gina's arm. "And if you're ever in trouble, you're more than welcome to seek refuge here at the store. We have a sitting room in the back with a refrigerator and coffeepot, and more than a few people have stayed a few days there over the years."

"Thank you so much!" Gina's eyes went shiny. "I appreciate your kindness." She fumbled at the phones in the display, picking up one, putting it back without looking at it and picking up another.

"This one's good. I've used these before." Buck identified a simple phone and pulled it off the rack.

"All right." Her voice was faint.

He was surprised that someone as competent and calm as Gina would get this upset over a piece of technology. "Look, it's just a phone," he said gently. "We can manage this."

"It's not just a phone!" She spun on him. "They're threatening… They want to…" She broke off, shook her head. "It's not just a phone," she repeated, her voice flat and dull.

"Here. We'll pay for it all together." But as Mr. Love rang up their purchases and Gina bit her lip, and her phone buzzed repeatedly, Buck was worried. So far, her former in-laws had taken away her transportation and her communication. What was next? Did they have no shame about mistreating the mother of their grandchild?

After a day of trying to drown her worries in work and avoid Buck's concerned glances, Gina hated to have to rely on him for a ride to pick up Bobby.

She'd realized a few days back that driving without a license could get her in trouble. Her license had been stolen along with her money, and she couldn't order a replacement without kicking all kinds of search engines into play. So when Buck and even Lacey offered her the use of their cars, she had to decline.

She disliked the lack of independence, would have tried hard to find a babysitter in town, except that Angelica's situation was so ideal: she was caring for her own baby and one other—gorgeous Amy Franklin's nephew—in a big, comfortable farmhouse. More important, Angelica was warm and loving and so, so good to Bobby.

Her own humiliation as she approached Buck, who was putting away plastering supplies, had to take a backseat to Bobby's well-being.

"Ready to go?" he asked, sparing her the need to ask. He was thoughtful that way. He seemed to anticipate what she might need and offer it, making it seem less of a burden and more of a friendly favor.

Still, the dependency rankled. "Yes, whenever you're ready, and thank you."

"No problem."

But when they arrived at the dog rescue

farm, Buck stopped her from emerging from the vehicle with a hand on her arm. "I feel like you're uncomfortable with accepting help. But that's what we do around here—we help each other."

She twisted her hands on her lap. "Why are you doing so much for someone you barely know?"

He opened his mouth and closed it, his eyes snagging with hers.

"What?" Her heart was pounding.

"You're worth it. I don't know who made you think you're not, but you deserve to be helped and treated well."

Those words were like a balm to Gina's soul, but she didn't completely trust them. "I'll go in and get Bobby and be right back out," she said, her breath coming fast. "Unless you want to come in? It's up to you."

"I'll come in and say hello." He was out of the truck and around to her side to help her before she could climb down herself.

They walked into an idyllic scene. On

the floor of the living room, all three babies sat, surrounded by toys. Amy's little one, Tyler, was shaking a rattle. Angelica's Emmie banged a truck on the floor, calling, "Ah-ah-ah." And Bobby sat up straight, staring at Emmie, the monkey in a circle toy in his hand forgotten.

On the comfortable couch, Amy and Angelica sat, keeping a relaxed eye on the babies.

Bobby saw Gina and waved his arms, a huge smile breaking out on his face. She picked him up and snuggled him to her. Even though this situation was obviously good for Bobby, it was hard to be away from him all day.

"Hey, Buck! Have we got a proposal for you!" Angelica glanced over at Amy and they both laughed.

"Why do I feel like I'm about to get talked into something?"

"We're having a girls' night," Amy said.

"And we want Gina and Bobby to stay."

"And we can drive them home after."

"So, thanks for bringing her out here, but—"

"We'd invite you to stay, but—"

Buck lifted his hands, palms out, and started backing away. "Hey, I get the message. I know when I'm not wanted."

At that moment, an ancient bulldog stood slowly from the dog bed where it had been resting and limped over to Buck. "See, Bull likes me even if nobody else does," he joked, squatting down to scratch behind the dog's ears.

Gina tried to feel upset that they hadn't even consulted her, just assumed she would stay, but truth to tell, she liked it. Liked feeling wanted, liked being around other women with babies. Liked having evening plans and something that felt like friendship.

Buck, though, noticed the omission and beckoned her over to where he was squatting beside Bull. "You want to stay or come on home? I'm fine either way."

"I'll stay." She felt absurdly conscious that she was planning her evening with him the way you would with a husband. "If that's okay with you, I mean, you drove me out here. But they said they'd bring me home..." She was babbling. She needed to stop babbling. She focused on Bobby, settling him back down on the floor beside the other babies.

"All right. See everyone later." With a final pat to Bull, Buck was gone.

Turning to face two women she didn't know well, Gina felt a moment of shyness, thrown back into a high-school world where, because of her dad's eccentric lifestyle and lack of money for stylish clothes, she hadn't fit in well with other girls. But Angelica stood and took her by the hand, tugging her toward the couch. "Here, hon, sit down. I'm just going to check on the salmon, and then we can pick up where we left off. You know Amy, right?"

"We're already friends," Amy said, and

Gina's heart warmed. "Bobby's so adorable." She tickled his chin. "Wow, how many teeth does he have?"

"Five, and I think he might be cutting another. He was super fussy last night."

"I hear you. That was us a week ago."

"You guys are having salmon? If I'd watched three babies all day, I'd barely be able to order pizza." Gina sat down on the couch next to Amy.

"She claims it's easy. And low calorie. And if we're good at dinner, we can eat the chocolate mud cake I picked up at the Chatterbox before I came out here."

Gina's mouth watered. "I am so there. I love chocolate. But what's the occasion?"

"Actually, we're second choice. Angelica was cooking for Troy and Xavier, but he'd forgotten to let her know they'd rescheduled a game for tonight. Basketball," she clarified. "Troy coaches. So she called me and asked if I'd bring dessert. I stopped by the café for three pieces of cake, and presto…it's a party.

I think she tried to call you, too, but couldn't get through."

That comment punctured Gina's pleasure. She pulled out her phone, looked at it. "I sent texts earlier today. In fact, I sent you a text, to see if we could get together this weekend."

"Didn't get it," Amy said. "Did you forget to pay your bill? Because when that happened to me once, I could text, or it seemed like it, but nothing sent and I couldn't receive messages or calls."

She'd sent the texts after the exchange with her in-laws, when they'd threatened to cut off her phone. So they had actually done it. That fast, she was severed from her old life. Suddenly, the salmon didn't smell so good. Her stomach churned.

The old bulldog came over and nuzzled at her hand, and she scratched his ears distractedly, trying to look on the bright side. She was actually slightly relieved that she wouldn't be getting texts or calls from her in-laws anymore. And she could give Angelica the number from her new, no-contract phone.

She could do this.

The only thing that worried her was, if they'd cut off her communication so quickly, would they come for Bobby next, as they'd threatened to do?

Amy was still looking at her quizzically, but Gina turned away, unsure of whether she could reveal any of her problems to these women she didn't know well. Fortunately, Angelica called them into the kitchen and they picked up the babies and went in.

"You have three high chairs?" Gina asked, surveying the neatly set table with chairs alternating with high chairs.

"I'm married to a Hinton," Angelica said wryly. "They have everything."

The farmhouse kitchen was warm and comfortable, even sporting a couch in the corner. They served themselves and chopped bits for the babies, and soon they were all digging in, talking like old friends. The kids babbled and guitar music played quietly in the background, and Gina felt her worries slide away.

"So," Amy said, turning to her purposefully, "I have an idea."

"What's that?"

"I want to rent a little space in downtown Rescue River, maybe start a craft and yarn shop."

"Wait a minute," Angelica said. "You're staying in Rescue River for sure?"

"It's a good place to raise Tyler, and I can't go back to New York." Amy didn't explain why. "With this craft shop, I'd like to link it in with the town's history. You're helping to restore Lacey's house and you know all about the historical-landmark stuff. Wonder if we could reclaim one of the old buildings in downtown and get grants to renovate it?"

Gina's eyebrows lifted. "That's an interesting idea," she said. "I've always dreamed of opening a shop for interior decorating, but I have no money to start something like that."

"That's why we need grants," Amy said. "I don't have a lot to invest, either, but I would guess a couple of the buildings on the edge of downtown are dirt cheap. Some of them may have historical significance. Isn't it worth checking them out?"

"Probably." Gina started to say more and then broke off. Could she be honest about her fears and limitations with these women?

She wanted so much to belong. To have true friends, not just acquaintances impressed with her fancy home and car.

But the more people who knew of her situation, the more likely someone would let slip some information that would lead her in-laws to Bobby.

She couldn't take that chance.

"I... Everything about my life is up in the air right now. I don't know how much help I can be." To avoid the pain of the cold shoulder that would inevitably follow, she turned to Bobby and helped him spoon up some food.

To her surprise, she felt a hand press her arm. "I understand problems," Angelica said. "When I came back to Rescue River, my life was pretty messed up."

From her other side, Amy sighed. "We all have issues. I don't know if I'll ever be able to be open about what happened to me in New York."

"Even if your problems are too big for you, they're not too big for God," Angelica said gently. "That's what I had to figure out before I could really be happy. Really open my eyes to what was around me, all the good stuff."

"Good stuff like Troy?" Amy teased gently.

"Exactly."

Gina felt some of the tension leave her shoulders. These weren't judgmental high-school girls; they were real Christian women, who weren't going to let the fact that someone didn't have a perfect life push them away.

Yet another reason she was glad she'd landed in Rescue River.

"Speaking of men," Angelica said, "what's going on between you and Buck?"

"You saw that, too?" Amy said to Angelica.

Her cheeks warming, Gina grabbed a wet cloth and focused on wiping off Bobby's hands and face. "Saw what?"

"It's not so much what I saw as what I felt," Angelica said.

"Vibes," Amy agreed. "Major emotional vibes between the two of you. And I was glad to see it. Buck's a nice guy."

"How long have you known him?" Angelica asked, and there was something in her voice, some guardedness that made Gina curious.

"We were in school together," Amy explained. "All through, from kids' birthday parties to high-school track to his goodbye party when he went in the service. Knew his family, knew Lacey. Loved his dad."

Angelica nodded. "From what I heard, everyone loved his dad."

"Didn't you know Buck, too?" Gina glanced

up from putting Bobby's sock back on. "You went to school here, right?"

"I was a year younger and on the outside of the main group in high school, but he was always nice to me."

"He's a good guy." Amy lifted her baby out of the high chair and took him over to the sink to wipe him down. "His mom had a pretty bad drinking problem, but Buck's dad and Buck and Lacey were so well liked, someone usually stamped down the gossip before it got too bad."

"It had its impact on Buck, though," Angelica said quietly. "Well, that and the war."

"So I hear." Amy came back to the table and sat down, holding Tyler on her lap. "I haven't been around for a few years, but wowie! The stories of his drinking reached me all the way in New York City."

"It was pretty bad." Angelica leaned back in her chair and looked at Gina, the skin between her eyebrows pleated. "One time before Troy and I got together…"

Gina lifted an eyebrow, waiting, her heart sinking.

"It's just… Buck and I were going to go out. He came out here—I was staying at the bunkhouse with Xavier. Anyway, he came to pick me up and he was really drunk. Too drunk to drive, so Troy and I called Lacey to come get him. He got pretty belligerent."

"I heard there were a lot of incidents like that," Amy said. "After he came back from Afghanistan, right? Substance abuse is a huge problem for vets. A way for them to cope with the things they saw and had to do."

Amy's choice of words—substance abuse—reminded Gina of how careful she needed to be. No judgment. She had absolutely no judgment where men were concerned.

She'd fallen for an addict before, and she was doing it again.

Angelica reached out and put a hand on Gina's arm. "I don't want to gossip, and I really like Buck. I'd just… I saw how you two were looking at each other, and I worried… Just be careful, okay?"

"Well, but he's in recovery, right?" Amy rocked Tyler gently. "That can really work. I saw it dozens of times out in California. And shouldn't we try to help him, not judge him?"

"Of course, and I feel for Buck—I really do. He's had so much to deal with." Angelica frowned. "It's just…sometimes recovery programs don't work. And families are devastated."

Gina knew about that firsthand. She nodded, her thoughts chaotic.

"I would never tell you what to do," Angelica said. "I'd just suggest you be careful. With Bobby and all."

Gina nodded. "I will." Restless, she stood and paced, Bobby on her hip.

On a built-in shelf beside the sink was a photograph in a wedding frame. Troy, Angelica and Xavier, all dressed up in wedding clothes, with the ripe harvest fields behind them.

Her throat closed. She remembered her own wedding day, the hopes, the promises. She'd thought that the biggest decision of her life was over and done. And done well.

There was so much she hadn't known on that day. So much suffering in the future.

But for someone like Angelica, who'd chosen the right man, the future *was* bright.

Amy and Angelica were still talking about Buck. "I just don't think he can handle a lot of stress. It's likely to push him back into drinking."

"That's so sad, but you're probably right."

"Troy says he plans to leave Rescue River as soon as he's repaid the debts he incurred during his drunk phase."

Gina gripped the edge of the sink as she listened and stared at the picture. No matter her romantic dreams, she and Buck weren't going to get together. There wasn't a potential relationship. She wasn't going to be saved by him.

She had to save herself…and leave Buck alone.

Chapter Eight

"So, why have you been avoiding me?"

The moment Buck asked the question, he wished he hadn't. He and Gina had to work together this whole evening—they'd set it aside to wallpaper after Bobby was in bed. She'd just come downstairs and into the front guest room. Lacey was away, working her third double shift this week.

"I haven't been avoiding you. We've been working together every day!" She stood by the table they had set up for spreading paste, her hand on her hip.

"Working together, yeah, but no talking. Did I do something wrong?"

He figured he knew the answer. It had started after her evening with Angelica and Amy. No doubt she'd been told some of the details about him and his past escapades.

She opened her mouth like she wanted to say something and then shut it again.

"Are you going to tell me or not?" He didn't know why he was pushing; it was like he'd lost control. Like when he'd been drinking, only he wasn't drinking. And he probably shouldn't make a big deal of it, but it was bugging him. The way she acted toward him mattered.

He definitely needed to discuss this with his sponsor.

She looked down, then lifted her eyes to his again. "It's just… I don't want you to get the wrong idea. We can't…you know."

He nodded, defeat blasting his heart. "You heard the truth about me." And he knew it, knew he had to get out of Rescue River for just that reason, but never had it discouraged him so much.

"It's not exactly that." She wasn't entirely denying it, he noticed, because she was honest to the core. "It's just…there *is* a spark." She lifted her eyes to his, looking troubled.

Heat rose in him at her words. "On your side or mine?"

She looked down, color staining her cheeks.

Was that because she felt the spark herself or because she didn't?

When she didn't answer, that told him everything. She'd noticed that he was attracted but she didn't feel the same herself.

In awkward silence they worked together to paste, lift and spread the wallpaper. The moments in between, while they were waiting for the paste to permeate the paper, felt uncomfortable. And when they got to the big break, when they had to let the whole room dry before putting the moldings back up, the silence was excruciating. He was just about to get up and go to his room when she spoke up suddenly. "Let's go explore the basement."

"What?"

"There's supposed to be a secret room or hiding place. Let's go try to find it."

Great. It was the last thing he wanted to do, the only way of breaking the silence he'd much rather have said no to.

But she was already out the door, and a gentleman couldn't let a lady go into the dark alone.

They made their way down the house's wooden cellar stairs. There was no railing, and a single bulb hung down to illuminate the old stone walls.

Something brushed his leg and he kicked out, barely restraining a yell, heart pounding.

An indignant yowl sounded, and the reclusive Mrs. Whiskers ran past him up the stairs.

Gina had grabbed a flashlight and she shone it around, but the darkness was so heavy that the light barely penetrated.

A sick feeling rose in him as they reached the low-ceilinged, dark main room, but Gina wasn't affected the same way; she was giggling, grabbing his arm at the scuttling sound of some little creature, shuddering openly. To her, it was obviously a trip through the fun house.

Sweat trickled down his back. He tried to focus on her and not on the memories.

"I wonder what's here. Have you even been down here before?"

"No." He could hear the hoarseness in his voice and wondered if she could, too.

"We'll go over the walls, see what we can find." She shone the light around, scanning the stone walls, exploring.

He took deep breaths of cold, dank air and told himself he was fine. He was in a basement in Ohio, not a cave in Afghanistan.

Still, when a rock she was fiddling with came out of the wall and fell to the floor with a thump, he grabbed her shoulders, heart racing, and pulled her back. "Come on. Let's get out of here."

She tried to move out of his grip, but he held on. "Come on!"

"Buck. Hey, Buck!" She twisted away but kept hold of his hand, shining the light in his direction. "Hey, what's wrong? You look awful."

He blew out a breath and drew in another lungful of musty cellar air. "Bad memories."

"Memories of what?" She tugged him over to where they could sit on the stairs.

Light came in from the open door above, illuminating an escape route. His breathing calmed a little. "Afghanistan. There were... lots of caves."

"And you had a bad experience in one." It wasn't phrased as a question.

"Yeah." He took another minute to breathe, feeling his body steady, his heart rate settle. He was cold from the sweat, but he no longer felt sick. And since he'd already wimped out on her, and since she didn't have any romantic interest in him anyway, he might as well tell her. "A buddy and I got ambushed in a cave. Separated from our unit, and we didn't know the country near as well as our enemies did. It got ugly." He ran a hand over his face.

"But you got out okay, in the end?"

"I did." A bleak sense of failure overwhelmed him.

"And your friend?"

He shook his head. "He didn't make it." And that was the shame of it. He should have been able to save John, but he hadn't. They'd made a plan to run for it, knowing they couldn't cover each other, but he should never have agreed to it, because John had gone down. And he'd never forget the misery of walking down off that mountain without his buddy.

"That must be hard to deal with." She'd never let go of his hand and now she gripped it tighter. "I can't imagine. Wow."

And then she just sat with him, quiet.

Her simple acceptance of how bad it had been, her comforting silence, surprised him. He hadn't told anyone—outside of his shrink—about that particular failure. He'd worried that he'd be condemned. Thing was, no one could condemn him more harshly than he condemned himself.

She was kicking at the bottom of the stairs and a loose board fell down. She picked it up and studied it.

"Look at that," she said.

"Is that a keyhole?" he asked at the same moment.

She squatted down and shone the flashlight under the stairs, and he had to marvel that she seemed to have no fear of mice or spiders or whatever other nasty thing could be down there.

Instead, she pulled out a wooden box, deteriorated, rotten on one side.

Her eyebrows lifted. She looked at him and then held it out.

He met her eyes and then, slowly, lifted the lid.

Inside was a tarnished silver cross necklace.

She studied it. "Wonder who this belonged to?"

"I don't know. Maybe there's some information in Miss Minnie's paperwork."

"Or maybe Mr. Love would know something."

He put the necklace back into the box and closed the lid. "We didn't find a secret room," he said, "but we found something interesting."

"There could be an amazing story behind this. We can display it in the guesthouse!" She sounded excited.

"You did the right thing, dragging me down here."

She looked at him and their eyes held. Hers sparkled with the excitement of their find and then darkened. Her tongue flicked across her lip.

It took everything in him not to kiss her.

"Buck?" she said faintly.

"Yeah?"

"It wasn't one-sided."

He lifted an eyebrow, wondering if she meant what he thought she meant.

"That…spark. I… I felt it. *Feel* it."

What was a man supposed to do when he'd faced his fears and found a treasure?

How was he supposed to remember to do the wise thing?

He put a hand on either side of her face, reading her expression, trying to figure out whether she'd mind. Her eyes were wide, but not afraid.

He pulled her closer and lowered his lips to hers.

Being in Buck's arms, immersed in his sweet but intense kiss, Gina felt like she was floating. Never in her life had she experienced anything like this.

His lips were firm. He definitely knew what he was doing, kissing her. She sighed and settled into the strong, warm circle of his arms.

He lifted his head to look into her eyes, and she couldn't hide her dreamy satisfaction. He nodded and dipped down for another kiss, his hands stroking and touching her back, but not straying anywhere that made her uncomfortable.

He was careful, protective. He was looking out for her rather than going for anything he could get. That alone set him apart from most men she'd known.

And the closeness she felt wasn't just physical. He wanted to know about her, to help her; he cared. More than that, tonight he'd let her know him more. What he'd revealed, his vulnerable side, made something burst free in her heart, a seed that could grow.

And then, through the baby monitor she'd left in the kitchen, she heard mild fussing.

"Bobby's crying," she told Buck.

He dropped his arms immediately. "Better check on him," he said, and she stood, steadied herself and then turned and hurried up the stairs, the little wooden chest still in her hand.

As she trotted up two flights, the euphoria of kissing Buck faded and doubts rushed in.

He's an alcoholic!

He's too vulnerable to take on the mess of your life!

He's leaving Rescue River!

She reached her room and found Bobby tossing, face red, half-asleep. He'd gotten himself into the corner of his crib and was too sleepy to find a more comfortable position.

She moved him and patted his back until he settled down.

Touching her baby brought her back into line with her goals. She needed to remember them.

She was here to take care of herself and Bobby, to protect her son from harm, and find a safe place to raise him.

She wasn't here to get involved with another risky, dangerous person.

The door creaked. "Is he okay?" Buck asked, coming up behind her, putting a hand on her shoulder.

A hand that felt possessive. And although everything inside her wanted to curl toward him, to feel his arms around her again, her responsibility for Bobby overcame it.

She braced herself. "That can't happen again," she said and looked up at him.

Hurt flashed across his handsome face, making her remember that he wasn't a care-free, blustering addict like Hank had been. He was a man who'd fought for his country and bore the emotional scars from it. A man who'd lost a wife and child.

She closed her eyes for just a minute, confused.

When she looked at him again, his mouth and eyes had gone flat. "All right. If you're both okay, I'm going to turn in."

His words were flat, too. When he walked away, his shoulders looked stiff.

Her mouth opened to call him back, and she pressed both hands over it to stop herself. It hurt to nip this thing between them, but it was best to do it now rather than ripping apart a full-grown love affair.

And it had to be stopped. It was best for Bobby. Ultimately, it was best for Buck, too.

But what about me? What about what I

want? She wrapped her arms around her middle. She felt like she was breaking apart.

When you were a parent, you made the decisions that were best for the child. That, she knew.

Doing the right thing was hard, but in the end, it would lead to less pain.

She walked over to her bed and sank down on it, arms still wrapped around her middle. She tried to pray, to cry out to God, but rather than finding comfort, she saw Buck's hurt face before her eyes.

Why did she have to hurt someone else to do the right thing by Bobby?

Why did she have to hurt herself?

No answers came. So, slowly, she closed the door to her room and got ready for bed. Went to check one last time on Bobby and saw the wooden box she'd been clutching in her hand when she'd run upstairs.

There was the cross. But now, studying the box in brighter light, she saw that it should be deeper than it was, suggesting that it had a false bottom. She tried to pry it up, and when her fingers wouldn't do the job, she found a metal nail file and slid it between the bottom of the box and the side, prying upward until the old piece of wood gave way.

Inside was a slim leather book filled with careful, old-fashioned handwriting.

Immediately, she thought of telling Buck. She wanted to share this with him. And she would, but not tonight—they were both too vulnerable, too hurt.

She flattened the pages out and began to read.

Buck paced the guesthouse, feeling like a caged dog. He picked up a magazine and then threw it down again. Started to straighten up the wallpapering supplies and then realized they'd just need to get them out again tomorrow. There was nothing to do now, and no way he was going to sleep.

He'd opened himself up to Gina, had experienced her sweetness and the hope of some more substantial connection with her.

But she'd shut him out.

He slammed a hand into the wall of the downstairs hallway and relished the pain of it. She'd responded to him; he was experienced enough to know that. Her breathing, her quickened pulse, her dark, lidded eyes told him that she'd enjoyed the kiss. And he hadn't pushed it too far; he'd been careful to respect her boundaries. He knew what kind of woman he was dealing with. Gina was a lady, through and through.

No, it was worse than that. When she'd gotten away from him and had had a moment to think, she'd realized she didn't want anything to do with him. What had she said? *No more of that.*

Maybe she'd had time to think about the drawbacks of a man who was afraid of small dark places. Or a man with a bad history everyone in town knew about. Or a man from a modest background, rather than the wealth she was accustomed to.

Or maybe it was just something about him.

For the second time this week, he thought back to his marriage. Not the loss of Ivana and Mia, but the months leading up to it, when he'd heard repeatedly about his failures and inadequacies as a husband.

He hadn't had it all together when he'd come back from Afghanistan. He'd needed counseling, time to figure out the right professional direction. The fact that he hadn't been sure of himself, combined with Ivana's weariness as a new mother, had made for stressful times.

It wasn't that he hadn't tried. He'd practiced listening skills he'd learned in counseling, brought flowers and gotten sitters so they could go out on dates. But none of it had worked.

You're not the man I thought you were. Those words, the ones he'd stuffed down and tried to forget, came ringing into his brain now.

He'd like to rip that brain right out of his skull. He could feel himself going down.

What did it matter if he had a drink, or ten? His life was never going to get any better. Work, sleep, try not to drink. Always alone.

At least at the bar, he'd have companionship. Not the kind he wanted, but something was better than nothing.

He paced some more. Looked up at the ceiling, where he could hear Gina moving around.

Was she upset, too? Uncomfortable hearing him roam around the house? Ambivalent about pushing him away?

Maybe she was, but she'd sounded sure of what she was saying. She'd made a decision.

Just for a moment, he'd thought he might get the girl. He'd thought that life could open up for him again, that he could have the companionship he craved. Not just someone to hold in his arms—although Gina fit beautifully there—but someone to talk to, someone who understood.

He had to get out of here.

Grabbing his jacket from the hook beside the door, he ran to his car and drove.

Twenty minutes later he was parking beside the big, dark barn out at the dog rescue farm. When he opened the door of his truck and slammed it shut, all the dogs started barking. Only then did he realize he needed to text Troy and Angelica, who lived with their kids in the adjacent house, to let them know he wasn't an intruder.

It's just me, out at the barn.

You okay? came the text back from Troy.

Yeah. Just forgot something.

He went inside, breathing in the familiar smells of hay and sawdust, feed and dogs. Rather than put on the main light, he just turned on the lamp on the desk near the door, found a flashlight and headed back.

The dogs continued barking, of course, and he got drawn into petting some of the needier ones. When he saw Spike, the Maltese mix from the alley the other day, he opened his crate, picked him up and carried him around. He'd turned out to be healthy enough, just your average senior, overweight dog with bad teeth. But with most of his matted hair shaved off, he was a little guy. He didn't fit in with the bully breeds that made up most of the population at the rescue.

"But somebody loved you, huh?" He rubbed behind the dog's ears, thinking of the note and the money.

The dog licked his face gratefully.

"Your breath smells worse than a garbage dump," he chided the old dog.

Yeah, he was talking to a dog. Which might mean he was crazy, or might mean he was sane.

Finally he got to the kennel he'd been seeking. There was Crater, in the back of it, licking his paws. When the dog saw Buck, he came bounding forward.

Buck opened the kennel awkwardly, still holding the Maltese. "Hey, buddy," he said. "Want to come home with me tonight?"

He only did that on the bad days. Lacey hadn't bargained for a big, clumsy dog in her house. But she knew he needed the company sometimes.

Crater trotted confidently beside him, mouth open, tongue hanging out. He seemed to laugh at the other dogs, still in their kennels.

When they got back to Spike's small crate, Buck bent down to put the little guy in.

Spike struggled, looking up at him with big, dark eyes, letting out pitiful cries.

"I don't even like small dogs." Firmly, he shut the crate and headed for the door.

Above the noise of the other dogs, he could hear Spike's high-pitched howl.

All the dogs were barking. All of them

needed a home. He was giving one of the unadoptables an outing, that was all. He reached down to rub Crater's head and the dog stared up at him adoringly.

That high-pitched howl again.

Buck groaned. Stopped. Started walking again.

Crater looked at him quizzically.

His steps slowed. He turned around. Then he jogged back to Spike's cage, opened it and swept the fat Maltese into the curve of his arm. "One night on a real bed. Just one, you hear?"

Twenty minutes later, as he let himself into the guesthouse and went upstairs—Crater beside him and Spike in his arms—he realized he hadn't even considered taking the turnoff for the bar.

Chapter Nine

A scratching sound tugged at Gina's consciousness. Was Bobby scratching, or was it Buck? Someone was in a box and she needed to help him get out of it, she knew that, but she couldn't make herself move.

More scratching, and then vigorous, high-pitched barking.

Barking?

And then an indignant yowl, some growling and more barking.

Gina sat up in bed, her eyes barely able to open. When she saw the bright daylight outside her window, she jumped up. How late had she slept?

Automatically she checked on Bobby, but he was sleeping through the sounds of an animal fight right outside their door. She shrugged into her robe and went out to see what was going on.

Buck was coming up the stairs at the same time, already dressed and covered with a fine white powder, like he'd been plastering.

"Hey." He snapped his fingers and the big dog, Crater, bounded over. Buck pointed at the floor, and Crater sat.

The orange cat, Mr. Whiskers, and his reclusive lady friend perched on a high, built-in ledge. They both glared disdainfully at a small, fat white dog who continued to bark furiously at them.

Gina bent down and picked up the little dog. It quieted down and licked her face before twisting toward the cats.

She wrinkled her nose. "Dog breath, wow!"

"His teeth aren't the best. That's Spike."

"Spike?"

"Uh-huh."

"Okay." She studied the ten-pound dog doubtfully. "These guys weren't here when I went to bed."

"I needed company," he said gruffly. "Sorry they woke you."

His words brought back the night before, and she immediately thought of their kiss. Her face heated and she started to touch her lips, then cuddled the little dog closer instead.

He'd needed company. Why had he needed company? Because she'd hurt him?

She remembered the old journal she'd found and opened her mouth to tell Buck about it when Bobby called. He was always hungry in the morning.

She pressed the little dog into Buck's arms and went to her son.

As she changed him and prepared him for the day, she heard Buck whistle to Crater and go back downstairs. Good. And she'd keep Bobby with her today, maybe do some paper-work instead of working beside Buck. They were making good progress on the renovation, and it looked like there would be several rooms ready to display for the festival if they all stayed on task. It was time to figure out a publicity plan.

And it was time for her to spend a day apart from Buck. Exactly what she *didn't* want to do, because the thought of working with him, beside him, filled her with longing. Made her want to share another sweet kiss.

But she couldn't reopen that wound. It was kinder to be cruel.

After feeding Bobby some breakfast, she went out onto the front porch. She sat on the steps and put a blanket and toys in the yard for Bobby. As he banged plastic together and plucked at grass, she updated the marketing plan.

At one point, Buck opened the door to let the little dog out and saw her there. "Will it bother you if Spike hangs outside with you? He's getting into everything." Buck's voice was toneless, exquisitely polite.

"No problem. I like him. C'mere, Spike."

Normally they'd have laughed together about the ill-fitting name. He'd have told her the dog's story. But today, he just nodded.

He was turning away when Bobby started shouting. "Buh! Buh!" He waved his arms at Buck and started to crawl toward him.

Buck looked back, and a muscle twitched in his jaw. He stepped inside and closed the door.

Pain twisted in Gina's chest. She didn't like being estranged from him. Didn't want this coldness. Didn't want Bobby to get sad from rejection, although truthfully, her son had spotted a robin and turned toward it, easily distracted.

If only she could be distracted that easily.

It's better this way. She tugged the little dog closer to her side and determinedly went on writing out her plan.

An hour later, she heard the sound of a camera clicking and looked up to see Amy, phone in hand, snapping photographs. "You just look so cute, with Bobby and that little dog," Amy said. "I'll send these to you. You working hard?"

"Yeah. Getting some paperwork done."

"For the national-landmark thing?"

She nodded as Amy opened the picket fence and let herself in. "Some of that, and I'm working on marketing. We need to send out some blasts on social media, get the word out about the guesthouse and how it'll be open for the festival."

"I can help with that," Amy offered. "You think you're going to make it, then?"

"It's looking good." Then it came together for her. "Hey, we need to take a bunch of pictures of the renovation. We can post them, and the fixer-upper crowd will think it's awesome."

"That's for sure. Want me to take a few more of the outside?"

"The inside, too, if you're willing. I'm a terrible photographer. But where's Tyler?"

"Out at Angelica's. Why isn't Bobby there today?"

"He's only there three days per week."

Gina didn't add that she needed the comfort of keeping her son close today.

They went inside and Amy walked around snapping photos. In the kitchen Gina put Bobby in his high chair, placating him with dry cereal while she fixed a tray of fruit, cheese and crackers for an early lunch. She made a separate plate for Buck to find when he was ready. She and Amy could sit outside to eat, away from him.

She could hear Buck and Amy talking, but she stifled her desire to listen. It didn't matter. Wasn't her business.

The voices came closer, and then they both walked into the kitchen. When Buck saw her, he stopped in the middle of a sentence. He stammered something, turned abruptly and left.

Amy frowned after him and then looked at Gina. "Why's the tension so thick in here?"

Gina so wanted to tell her. She was suffering from a serious shortage of girlfriend consultation.

But what could she say? *He kissed me and*

I liked it and then I cut him off? It'll never work for me because of who he is and who I am? I'm crazy about him?

She blew out a sigh. "Grab those glasses, will you? I'll carry the pitcher and we can have some lunch outside."

Once they were settled on the porch, Gina rocked Bobby and held him against her, and just as she'd hoped, he relaxed into sleep. After he drifted off, she ate some snacks with one hand and held him, and then Amy made a nest for him and they laid him down.

"You're still not off the hook. What's going on between you and Buck?"

Unable to think of a real excuse, Gina settled for half the truth. "We went forward a little bit in our...friendship. And then we... I...decided not to go further."

"Why?" Amy poured another glass of lemon-infused water for both of them.

"Because Bobby comes first," Gina said firmly.

"And? Is Buck somehow anti-Bobby?"

"No, he's great with him. It's just…men mostly aren't reliable, and Buck…well, you heard what Angelica said that one night. He's got a drinking problem, and I—"

"He's in AA, right?" Amy interrupted. "Have you ever seen him drink?"

"No, I've never seen him drink. But still…"

"Why did you say men mostly aren't reliable?"

Man, Amy was like a bloodhound on the scent. But Gina didn't know whether to get into talking about her dad. "Just…past history."

"But Bobby's a boy. It would be nice if he had some male role models in his life."

"That's true, and yet…" She sighed. "I don't know." She leaned over to check on Bobby, hoping Amy would take the hint and get off this line of questioning.

But no chance of that. "What was your childhood like?" Amy pressed. "Was your dad in the picture?"

"Yes." Gina thought of her dad, and as

always, the shaggy, smiling image of him brought a fond feeling. "He was my only parent. My mom passed on right after I was born."

"Good relationship with him, I assume? Because you're smiling."

"I'm smiling because I love him to pieces," Gina said. She was about to stop there, to brush it all off as she usually did with inquiries about her childhood, but Amy's understanding face, her receptive silence, made Gina feel like she could share a few details. "But my childhood was a little different."

"Different?"

Wondering how to explain, Gina thought back, and a memory flashed into her head. "Once when I was about seven," she said, "I invited a couple of girls to come over after school. We all got notes from our parents and they rode home on the bus with me." She put her elbows on her knees and leaned forward, remembering. "When we got off the bus, we were running up toward the house, but one of the girls stopped. She wanted to know why my house was so little, and why the porch roof was sagging, and why the driveway was made of dirt, not asphalt."

"You grew up poor," Amy guessed.

"Yeah. I explained it away, and we went inside. And there was nobody home."

"Your dad was gone?"

She nodded. "I was used to being alone, but they both got scared and started to cry. They wanted their moms."

"What did you do?" Amy asked.

"I fixed us all a snack. Showed them how to put butter and sugar on white bread, and they loved it. And then I told them stories until their moms came to get them."

Amy nodded, looking sympathetic and nonjudgmental. "Sounds like you were pretty mature. Did the moms find out?"

"My dad rolled in just as they did, and somehow, he smoothed it over. He really was handsome back then, and super articulate. There wasn't a woman within miles who couldn't be charmed by him." She sighed. "But of course, the girls weren't allowed to come over again, and they spread the word. Pretty much nobody trusted my dad to do what he said he'd do."

Amy nodded. "And so you don't trust men," she said. "Makes sense, with that background."

Gina hadn't really put it together like that before, and she wasn't sure she bought it. "I got married, though. I was happily married." For a while.

"And what was he like? Your husband."

Gina thought. "He was the playmate I never had," she said, her eyes filling with tears. "When we were first dating, and when we first got married, we had so much fun together. He really *was* like a little boy, and I got to be a kid again with him, too."

"That sounds good," Amy said, "but it also sounds like you married your father. Someone else irresponsible, you know? How did he do when Bobby came along?"

Gina frowned. "Not well. I couldn't party anymore, and he couldn't cope with responsibility, and…" She blew out a sigh. How to explain the disaster their marriage had become? How to explain the issues with his parents, who'd morphed from kindly caregivers to monsters with the arrival of Bobby?

She pushed her plate away. "I should probably get back to work. I'm sorry to do all that talking."

"It's okay," Amy said. "I was the one asking all the nosy questions."

"I'm glad you came over." And she was. Gina hadn't had much girl talk since she'd been here, aside from a couple of phone calls with Haley back in California.

They hugged, and then Amy held her shoulders. "Remember," she said, "the past doesn't have to determine the future. Buck isn't your dad. And he's not Bobby's father. Give him a chance, okay?"

Except he was all too much like them, Gina thought as she settled back down to work.

And though she'd put her trust in two men who hadn't repaid it, she wasn't going to make the same mistake a third time.

She watched her baby's chest rise and fall with his sleep breathing. No mistakes. Not this time. The stakes were too high.

After lunch, Buck changed into scrubs and headed out the front door, Crater trotting behind him.

Gina still sat there, working on Lacey's laptop. Bobby slept beside her and the little Maltese pressed against her side. In the spring sunlight, she looked so pretty that his throat hurt.

He swallowed. "C'mon, Spike. Time to go back to jail."

"Do you have to take him?" She put a protective hand on the dog.

"We're not set up for a dog here." He looked around, anywhere but at her. "No little-dog food, no dog bed..."

"I know, but he looks so sad!"

As if to prove her point, the dog peered

up at him from beneath shaggy fur, his dark eyes pleading.

"I know—that's why I brought him home. But Lacey..." His sister hadn't okayed it. She also was never home these days; she was working double shifts at the hospital, ostensibly to earn extra cash, but really, probably, to stay away from the painful memories Bobby evoked.

"Oh, of course. I wasn't thinking." She sat up straighter, scooped the dog off the wicker couch beside her and deposited him into Buck's arms.

The dog whined and struggled to get back to Gina.

"Hey, come on, buddy." He scratched behind the dog's ears until it settled into his arms as if confident he'd do the right thing.

Gina was watching him expectantly, too.

"Okay, look, I'll work on it. But no promises."

"Of course!" She was beaming. "Thank you!"

Buck would do just about anything to

make her smile like that again. Which was really bad.

It was almost like he was falling in love with her.

Stuffing down that very disturbing thought, he spun away and hurried down to his truck.

Out at the rescue, after Buck had put Crater and Spike back into their kennels, he and Troy did a couple of procedures, working together like a well-oiled machine. Buck prepped and assisted, grateful for the distraction from his troubled thoughts.

One of the local farmers brought in a goat that had gotten tangled in some barbed wire, and Buck cleaned and bandaged its leg. In town, Troy's practice was mainly small animals, but out here, they did what was needed.

Spike barked and whined every time he walked by, so when they hit a lull and were doing paperwork in the office, he brought the Maltese out and let it run around. After a cursory sniff of the room, the dog settled beside Buck's office chair.

"What's up with that?" Troy asked, nodding toward Spike. "Thought you went for bigger dogs, like Crater."

"Yeah. He's just so…" Buck trailed off and reached down to scratch the shaggy little guy's ears.

"Needy?"

"Yeah."

Troy nodded and changed the subject abruptly. "How are Gina and Bobby doing?"

"Great, I guess." Buck focused on the intake form in front of him, filling in the details.

Troy leaned back in his office chair and put his hands behind his head. "You guess? Thought you'd know."

Buck shook his head and kept on writing.

"I thought something was heating up between you."

"No." Buck looked up to meet Troy's assessing gaze. "Can't."

"How come?"

Impatiently, Buck gestured toward himself. "Look at me, man. I'm a mess. Not a good choice for anyone."

"I don't know about that. Your life is more stable than hers."

Stable wasn't a word Buck had applied to himself, ever. But if he thought about how he lived now, he realized, it was accurate. He stayed with his sister, went to work at one or the other of his jobs, came home, went to bed. Got up and did it all again. Even went to church on a regular basis, and got something out of it.

But he'd seen the expression in Gina's eyes after that night she'd gotten together with Angelica and Amy, and then again after they'd kissed. She'd heard things. She had doubts about him, and understandably so. "I have a history, and it keeps wanting to chase me."

"People see you changing," Troy said mildly. "You're not chained to your past."

Buck stood, restless. It was what Dion had said, too, but he and Troy were both looking at life with rose-colored glasses. The past *did* come back to bite you. "I gotta get back, do a little more work tonight." He paused then, fingered his sobriety coin and made an abrupt decision. "Hey, listen. You know I'm working the steps in AA."

Troy nodded.

This was never easy. "One of the steps is making amends, and I need to do that with you."

Troy tipped back in his chair. "You're doing great now. That's all that matters."

"No." Buck forced himself to stand there and go through with it. "I was a jerk in a number of ways, but a day I remember in particular, I came in to assist with surgery when I'd been drinking. Started to botch things up, and you had to kick me out and finish it all yourself."

"I remember. I think I had a few choice words for you."

"I deserved them. I put the dog you were working on at risk, and I'm sorry." As soon as he said that, a weight he hadn't known he'd been carrying lifted off his heart. "I'd like to find a way to make that up to you."

Troy let his chair fall forward with a gentle bang. "You don't owe me anything. But—"

he waved an arm toward the dog area "—you might owe something to those guys. Or, at least, to one of them." He looked down at the Maltese that stood patiently at Buck's feet. "Think about it."

"I will." He shrugged into his jacket and headed for the door. Spike trotted confidently after him. When he started to go outside, the dog ran out and jumped at Buck's truck.

Afternoon sun heated Buck's back, and a cardinal sang its "Birdie? Birdie? Birdie?" from the top of a bare-limbed tree. Buck took a minute to breathe in the spring air.

Troy stood in the barn's doorway, watching as Buck walked to the truck, opened the door and lifted the little dog in.

"Hey," Troy called. "The half-drunk guy who used to stumble in here wouldn't have given that dog a second glance," he said. "You're changing, whether you know it or not."

"He's crazy, right?" Buck said to the little dog as he put the truck in gear.

The dog propped its front legs on the door to look out, making nose smears all over the side window. Buck sighed, lowered the window a little so the dog could at least catch a whiff of springtime and drove back to the guesthouse at a sedate pace that wouldn't knock the Maltese down.

Troy was right. On days like this, Buck barely recognized himself.

Chapter Ten

Two days later, Gina was drinking a glass of lemonade on the porch, trying to muster the energy to either cook dinner or take Bobby to the park, when a shuffling sound drew her attention to the street.

Miss Minnie Falcon was approaching the house, pushing her walker. She stopped in front of the gate and shaded her eyes with her hand, looking up toward the house.

"I'll get it, Miss Minnie," Gina called. She hoisted Bobby to her hip and hurried down to open the gate. "Would you like to come up and sit for a while?"

"I would, thank you. I'll just leave my

trusty steed here." She parked her walker beside the porch steps.

Gina laughed, helped her up the steps and into an upright rocking chair and then brought her a glass of lemonade.

Bobby crawled over and pulled up on Gina's leg, looking curiously at Miss Minnie.

"Why, look at him stand right up!" the older woman said. "Is he walking yet?"

"So far, he likes crawling better. It gets him around faster." Gina replaced the baby gate at the top of the porch steps and handed Bobby the colorful roll-and-crawl ball they'd gotten from Buck's stash. Bobby batted it, chortling when a tune started to play and then crawling after it. "I feel like he's ready to walk. He cruises all around holding on to things, but he just hasn't done it by himself yet."

"Everything in its own time. Once he starts to walk, you won't be able to hold him back." Miss Minnie leaned forward and took a sip of lemonade. "My, this is delicious. Thank you, dear. I won't bother you for long."

"It's no bother. Truthfully, I'm glad for the company." Gina meant it, too. Not only because she'd been feeling a little lonely, but because it was mostly the older generation who shared her fascination with history. "In fact, I'd love it if you'd tell me something about this house. Were you born here?"

Miss Minnie nodded and relaxed back into the chair. "Oh, yes. I was born here and lived my whole life here. My parents wanted to fill it with children, you see, but there was only me. I did have a lovely childhood, though. Right here in the middle of town, everyone stopped by."

"It's a perfect location," Gina agreed.

"Everyone from all the farms would come to do their Saturday shopping in town, and of course, they came Sunday for church, so we always had something going on." Miss Minnie looked off into the distance as if she were able to see the past. "Father passed when I was in my twenties. But Mother lived to be quite old. Almost as old as I am now." Miss Minnie looked down at herself and chuckled, then shook her head. "I'd bring her out onto the porch every day and we would have a little tea before dinner. She loved to watch the people go by."

Gina smiled and nodded, hoping the older woman would continue. "Has Rescue River changed much?"

Miss Minnie gestured toward town. "The Chatterbox Café has been here for as long as I can remember. Lyman's Tailors and Sadie's Stout Shop are gone. But Love's Hardware, that's still there."

"I met Mr. Love last week."

"Oh, that man." Miss Minnie shook her head with a little smile.

Gina suddenly remembered Buck's comment that Mr. Love was sweet on Miss Minnie. "He seemed charming," she said, lifting an eyebrow.

"Indeed he is." Two high spots of color

appeared in Miss Minnie's cheeks. "Now, that's enough about me. Tell me, child, are you planning to stay here in town?"

Gina looked around at the sunny street and sighed. "I love it here. But I only have my job of helping with the renovation a couple more weeks, until the Freedom Festival." Something about Miss Minnie's inquisitive, sparkling eyes made Gina want to confide. "It's hard for Lacey, having Bobby here. He reminds her of all she lost." Although to be fair, Lacey had been trying to get comfortable with Bobby, asking Gina questions about him and even, a time or two, offering to hold him.

"Of course." Miss Minnie shook her head. "That poor child, she's had so much heartache. As has her brother."

"But…it's strange. Buck seems to like babies, even though he lost his daughter."

"Men and women are different." Miss Minnie set down her lemonade and rocked gently. "Although I never had children myself, I know how women hold on to things. And then Lacey's husband…" She rocked faster for a moment, shaking her head. "Well. I'm not about to spread gossip." She looked at Gina with curiosity. "Some folks seem to think you and Buck Armstrong make a good couple."

Heat rose to Gina's face, revealing too much, and she laughed weakly. "Oh, well…"

Miss Minnie's face crinkled into a smile and she patted Gina's arm. "Let an old woman give you some advice. Life is short, and the things you think will always be there one day are gone." She looked around at the porch and the house, her chin trembling a little. "One day, everything's gone."

Gina's throat tightened. Not sure of what to say, she reached out to squeeze Miss Minnie's hand. "I'm so glad you came over. I'd like to hear more about the house and its history."

Buck's truck pulled into the driveway, and a minute later, he trotted up the stairs, holding the little white Maltese that had made its way into Lacey's heart by now, as well as Buck's and Gina's. "Hey, Miss Minnie, how's it going?" he asked cheerfully.

"Well, I declare, this house is Grand Central station." The elderly woman's voice was cheerful again. "And my mother would turn in her grave to know there were dogs living here."

"He's just a visitor," Buck said, "but if I remember right, you and your mother were all about cats." He opened the door and whistled, and the orange tabby walked out, tail high.

"Now, is that Mister or Missus?" Miss Minnie asked.

"It's Mister. Can't you tell he's a tough guy?" Buck picked up the cat in his free hand, chuckling, and deposited him in Miss Minnie's lap.

After they'd visited a few minutes more, Miss Minnie petting the purring Mr. Whiskers, the older woman headed back to the Senior Towers.

Gina fixed a quick dinner and they made short work of the dishes. Gina settled Bobby in his crib and then, feeling more comfortable with Buck for the first time since their kiss, came back downstairs. "Do you have time to look at something?" she asked Buck.

"Sure." He looked surprised but not unhappy that she'd reached out to him.

She showed the box and the journal to Buck. "This journal was in the box we found."

He studied the first pages. "Who wrote this? One of Miss Minnie's relatives?"

"I read the whole thing," Gina said, "and I think it was written by a young fugitive woman who stopped here on the way north."

"Really?" Buck examined the pages with more interest. "That's some history."

"Read it!"

She watched as Buck turned slowly through the old pages, deciphering the spidery handwriting, getting as caught up as she had herself at the tale of Minerva, a young fugitive who'd fallen in love with Abraham Falcon, the eighteen-year-old son of the Falcon family.

He looked up at one point, shaking his head. "He proposed? And gave her a fancy ring? That must have raised some eyebrows pre–Civil War."

"Apparently so. Especially since she was expecting a baby. But the people who were most upset were those she'd escaped with. They didn't think Abraham—or any white man—could be trusted."

"Understandable." He read a little more. "So they tried to talk her out of it and she wouldn't listen."

"Right, and wouldn't come along as they were getting ready to go to the next station."

"Which was the Old Rose Barn, I guess? Mr. Love's family place?"

"It must have been. It's not very far away, but I was reading that stations were pretty close together in this area." Gina was glad

Buck was as interested in the story as she was. "Apparently, she didn't trust Abraham completely, because she concealed the fact that she could read and write. When he found out, he was angry she'd concealed it, and she was angry that he couldn't understand why."

Buck whistled. "*I* can understand it. Teaching a slave to read and write was a crime in the old South. She'd probably had to conceal her ability for years."

"Anyway," she said, too impatient to wait for him to read the whole journal, "they had a big fight. Minerva got mad and gave the ring to her sister as she was leaving. She told her sister to use it to get to freedom. But her sister said no, she'd hide it in the roses for Minerva to find when she got over being angry."

"If she was that mad at Abraham, why didn't she go along with the others?"

"She said she knew it would slow everyone down. She was near her time of giving birth."

"So did they make up, Minerva and Abraham?" Buck had given up all pretense of reading the diary for himself.

"They did. The last entry is about how happy she is that they've come to understand and trust each other even better than ever before."

"The last entry? So we don't know what happened?" His forehead wrinkled as he turned to the last page. "It just stops. There was no ring with the journal, no description of a wedding?"

She shook her head. "She must have started another journal, or else been busy with the baby. At least, I hope that's what happened. I hope she didn't have to give up on marrying him."

Buck nodded. "Totally understandable that her friends didn't want her to trust Abraham."

"But she believed in him."

A curious expression crossed Buck's face and then was gone. "I wonder what roses she's talking about. Where her sister hid the ring, and whether Minerva and Abraham ever found it."

"She said she'd hide it in the roses. I wonder if that was around here? The roses couldn't still have survived, I don't think."

"I don't know," he said. "There's a rose garden right by the sign coming into town..."

"Oh, there are a million possibilities, and this journal is really old. We probably wouldn't find anything now." Gina felt disappointed. "At any rate, mementos like the journal should be preserved."

"Since Abraham is one of her ancestors, Miss Minnie may know what happened to them, whether they got married," Buck said. "Or maybe Mr. Love will. He's also familiar with the town's history." He studied the ragged, leather-bound book again. "This reminds me of hunting for treasure when I was a kid."

"Hey, I have an idea," Gina said without thinking it through. "We should go digging."

"Are you asking me out?" he shot back.

And then he blew out a breath. "Sorry. I know you're not."

She looked into his eyes and read the confusion there. She was confused, too. She'd made the decision that he should not be in her life, and she hadn't had a moment's happiness since. "You don't need to be sorry."

"No. I *am* sorry. We can't go there. I'm leaving, and you're focused on Bobby. It's fine."

The thought of him leaving crushed her happy feelings. She was lonely, plain and simple. Bobby was wonderful, but he was a baby. She was starting to make some friends, but that didn't fill the gap in her.

"Tell you what," he said. "After Bobby goes to sleep, and Lacey's home in case of any problem, let's go out searching."

"You mean it?" If they were going to be apart, a little time together wouldn't be bad. Would it? Especially if there was a mystery involved?

And the idea of a mystery sparked another thought. "I wonder if we could also look at Miss Minnie's old materials about the house," she said. "We might find answers there. And we might find some stuff that would make awesome decorations for the guesthouse. We can have cases and shadow boxes. Guests will love knowing more about the history of the place."

He was looking at her, smiling. "You don't do things halfway, do you?"

She flushed. "Just stop me. I'm getting carried away again."

"No need to stop. I like it."

High-pitched barking from the ground broke their gaze. Spike, wanting attention.

"Hey, buster, don't be jealous," Buck said to the concerned little dog. And then to Gina: "Meet me here after Bobby's asleep?" He touched her hair, pulled his hand back with a wry grin and then disappeared up the stairs, Spike trotting behind him.

When the doorbell rang around eight o'clock that night, Buck was knee-deep in plaster supplies, but he wiped his hands off and tried to get downstairs before whoever it was rang again. This was about the time Gina put Bobby down, and Buck didn't want to wake him up.

Didn't want anything to interfere with their plans for later. Idiot that he was.

But when he got there, Gina was already at the door.

She listened, opened the door to take a business card and then opened the door wider to let the person in.

Danny Walker.

Local banker and resident womanizer.

"Come on in the kitchen," she said. "We can talk in here." She led him toward the kitchen, only belatedly noticing Buck standing there in the hallway, clothes a mess compared to Danny's nice suit.

"Hey!" Danny held out a hand and pumped Buck's. "I heard you were living here, working on the place. That's just great, what you and Lacey are doing here."

"Thanks. What's up?" In his not-that-friendly voice was the question *Why are you here?*

"Got some business to talk over with Gina here," he said easily.

Buck cocked his head.

Gina lifted an eyebrow at him. Her message was plain: *not your affair.*

And she was right. It wasn't. He stomped back upstairs and applied plaster with extra energy, then did some repairs downstairs until, finally, he heard Danny leave.

It took him about thirty seconds to think of an excuse to go into the kitchen. And then he wished he hadn't, because Gina was smiling.

"What did he want?" he asked.

"He wants my business," she explained happily. "He'd heard about my interest in possibly starting an interior-decorating place, and he wanted to talk about loans and options."

Buck frowned skeptically. "Do you really think it was your *business* he was after at eight at night?"

"What else?" She looked puzzled.

"Maybe…to hit on you? You're a beautiful woman."

Gina didn't seem to love the compliment. "So the only thing I have going for me is my looks? Nobody would want my ideas or my creativity or the work I can do?"

"I didn't mean that. It's just… I know Walker. He has a track record."

"Thanks a lot for undermining my confidence." Gina shoved back her chair and started noisily putting dishes away. "He was totally respectful and businesslike. I'm meeting him for coffee next week to talk more about it."

"There you go. He was after a date and he got it."

"It is *not* a date! Every outing isn't a date!" She came closer and stuck her finger in his chest. "And what's more, I don't appreciate your stomping around upstairs, or pounding nails in the next room, when I'm trying to have a business meeting!"

It had been obvious, then. And even though he knew that Danny wouldn't have called on a homely woman with such alacrity, he still felt bad. "I'm sorry. I guess I'm jealous."

She'd turned away with a flounce, but at his words, she spun back. "Jealous? Of what?"

Now he was truly and deeply in it. He studied the toe of his work boot, scraped it across the floor. "Of a guy who might be hitting on you. Wanting to date you."

"We've already discussed how nothing can happen between us, Buck!" She crossed her arms over her chest, looking exasperated. "So even if I *did* want to go out with this Danny guy—which I don't—I don't see where you'd have a leg to stand on, being jealous."

"I know," he said miserably. "It's true. I'm sorry."

She had opened her mouth to say something, but now she shut it. "You're sorry?"

"I was wrong," he added. "I shouldn't have

come in here or asked you anything about it. Or banged around while you were talking to him."

She laughed and rolled her eyes. "When you apologize so well, how can I stay mad at you?"

It was like the sun came out again. "So, you still up for hunting treasure?"

"As soon as Lacey gets home, as long as she agrees to keep an ear open for Bobby. He shouldn't wake up—he was exhausted, but there's always a first time. She can call me and we won't be far away."

Lacey came in the door just then, wearing scrubs, looking tired. "Hey," she said, waving to them. "You two look like you're up to something."

Gina explained about the journal and showed it to Lacey, quickly explaining their quest. Watching them together, Buck was guardedly optimistic. Lacey seemed to have come around to where she liked Gina, and she was doing better with Bobby, paying him a little bit of attention, giving in to his cute ways.

And now Lacey said she was willing to listen for Bobby, even asking Gina to put her baby monitor in her room. "Because I'm just grabbing a sandwich and going to bed. I want to make sure I hear him."

So the women organized that while Buck got cleaned up. He and Gina both emerged from their rooms at the same time, and Buck was absurdly pleased that she'd put on a pretty skirt and sweater. He'd worn khakis himself, something different from his usual scrubs and jeans.

All of a sudden, holding the door for her and walking down the porch steps beside her, Buck felt like he *was* on a date. Even after all their discussions to the contrary.

They strolled through the darkened downtown, gently lit by old-fashioned streetlights. There was a March chill in the air, belying the day's earlier springlike weather. A family headed into the Chatterbox Café. Someone emerged from Love's Hardware, and then the illuminated sign clicked off.

Gina shivered and pulled her jacket tighter, and Buck wanted to put an arm around her and pull her close. Wanted it so much that he pressed his arm tight against his side to make sure he didn't slip up and do it.

When they passed the Ace Tavern, it served to remind him of why he shouldn't make any move toward a relationship with Gina.

As they got to the edge of the town, traffic thinned out, pedestrian and vehicular. Finally they reached the Rescue River sign, on a little garden spot with a bench and some bushes, and Buck pulled out the canvas bag of gardening tools he'd brought.

"I remember when I first saw this sign," Gina said. "It seemed like a fantasy, that I'd ever be welcome and safe. But I do feel that way now."

"I'm glad," he said and risked taking her hand to tug her over to the bench. "We'd better wait until full dark. I doubt digging up the ground around the town's welcome sign is smiled upon."

She hesitated and then sat down beside him, and this time, he couldn't resist putting an arm along the back of the park bench. It was there, for her to lean into or not.

She did, and nothing felt so natural as to tighten his arm around her.

They sat and talked as the stars peeked out and the moon rose, its silvery light casting shadows. When she shivered, he pulled her tighter against him, but the way her closeness tugged at his heart, the confusing little sigh she let out, made that seem like a bad idea. "We should dig," he said, forcing briskness into his tone. "We don't have all night. You'll get frostbite."

She laughed but stood and walked around, looking at the little plot of land. "If I were hiding a romantic memento, I'd hide it… here."

"Under the sign?"

"Yep. According to Miss Minnie, there

was always a little garden here, welcoming people to town."

"But the sign wasn't here back in the day," he argued, just for the sake of talking to her, hearing her voice. He knelt down where she'd indicated, though, pulled out a shovel and started to dig.

"It should be under the rosebush, if that's a rosebush," she said. "Are you finding anything?"

"I don't… Wait. I'm hitting something, but it's probably just a rock."

He dug a little more and was about to pull a giant stone out when headlights illuminated them.

Gina clutched his shoulder and he stood quickly, stepping in front of her. Adrenaline surged in him, but not the crazy kind. This was Rescue River, not Afghanistan.

"Not the criminals I expected." It was Dion's deep voice. Behind him was his black-and-white police car.

"Hey, man." Buck reached out to grasp the

chief's hand. "Thanks for not using the siren on us."

"What are you two doing?"

"We're trying to solve a mystery," Buck explained. "Show him the diary, Gina."

She fumbled in her purse and brought it out, encased in a large plastic bag, and they took turns telling the big police chief an abbreviated version of the story it contained.

Dion shone his light down on the book, looking thoughtful. Then he turned the flashlight on the hole Buck was digging. "You find anything?"

"We thought we might find the ring her sister hid. It was supposed to be among the roses." He shook his head. "Hit something down there, but I'm pretty sure it's a rock."

"Are we in trouble?" Gina asked at the same moment.

Dion chuckled. "As crimes go, this isn't the worst. I might let you off with a warning if you fill up the hole all nice."

"You never heard about anything hidden here?"

Dion frowned. "I've been in Rescue River a long time. I've heard a few things, but not about here."

"Where, then?"

He studied them thoughtfully as if trying to decide whether to tell them. Finally, he nodded. "You ever been to the old cemetery?"

"The one by the church? That's the only one I know about," Buck said.

"No. There's another one. I'll show you."

After they'd filled in the hole and replaced the sod, Dion drove them out one of the country roads to a tumbledown church. Behind it was an overgrown yard with multiple depressions and a few stones. "This is a cemetery?" Gina asked, stepping closer to Buck.

"It's the AME cemetery," he said. "Not used anymore, but some folks still have kin buried here. And look." He led them across the rutted ground and to a stone bench that backed up against the woods. "Know what that is?" he asked, touching a tangle of vines that grew as tall as he was.

Buck shook his head.

"Is it…a rosebush?" Gina guessed.

"That's exactly what it is. I wonder if what's referred to in your journal is buried here."

Buck studied the bench and the bush. "Could be."

"Have a look around, but don't dig. We don't want to disturb anyone's remains."

Gina knelt in front of the little bench, looking at the rosebush, its buds just starting to come out. "What a lot of history is here," she whispered, touching the carving there.

Dion shone his powerful flashlight on a couple of stones next to the bench.

"'A friend loves at all times,'" Buck read from one of them. "Proverbs 17:17."

"Look at this," Gina said, kneeling to trace the inscription on a nearby headstone. "Minerva Cobbs. She didn't write her last name in the diary, but could this be her grave? How many Minervas could there be in a town the size of Rescue River?"

"Are there dates?"

"No. And if this is her grave, she didn't change her name to Abraham's." Gina bit her lip. "I did an online search for Minerva Falcon and nothing came up. I really wonder what happened."

They looked around a little while longer but didn't find a ring or anything else that would help fill in the blanks of the story, a story Buck was getting curious about himself. Or maybe he just wanted to keep that interested sparkle in Gina's eyes. "How are we going to find out the rest of it?" he asked her.

"Talk to the old folks," Gina said promptly. "They're more likely than anyone to know. Are you in?"

Dion raised an eyebrow, his mouth quirking a little at one corner.

"I'm all in," Buck said. Right or wrong,

he wanted to spend every moment he could with this woman. Every moment he had before leaving town.

Chapter Eleven

The next week went by in a flurry of renovations. They worked hard to get the first floor ready for the Freedom Festival, and when the Monday before the festival arrived, Gina could look around the guesthouse and feel assured that what she'd promised Lacey would come to pass. They'd be ready.

She and Buck had postponed their meeting with Mr. Love and Miss Minnie, but this morning, as they returned from dropping Bobby at Angelica's place, they settled on the next day.

"Should we take them out to lunch?" Gina

asked. "I know Miss Minnie likes to go to the café."

Buck turned down the road into town. "If we want to look at Miss Minnie's materials, maybe we should meet at the Senior Towers."

"Great. If you can pick up Mr. Love, we'll meet there right after lunch." They were driving through downtown. "Speaking of the Chatterbox, can you drop me off there?"

"Sure." He pulled up beside the place, and Gina told herself she didn't need to provide Buck with an accounting of her day, where she was going or whom she was with.

At the same time, they'd gotten in a rhythm of working together. "This shouldn't take long," she said, "and I'll be back at the house to work on that crown molding."

"Take your time," he said, his voice expressionless. "There's your breakfast date, right there."

"It's not a date!" She gathered her purse and briefcase and slid out of the truck without waiting for Buck to get the door for her.

Nonetheless, he got out and stood beside the truck, for all the world like a protective father. She rolled her eyes.

"Gina!" Danny greeted her happily. "Come on—I've got us a table." He nodded at Buck and escorted Gina inside, a hand on the small of her back.

When Buck did that, she liked it. But when Danny did it, it felt...creepy. She walked faster to get some distance from his touch.

As they sat down to discuss more details about a possible loan, Gina felt uneasy. Why *did* Danny need to meet with her again? And why were they doing it at a restaurant instead of at the bank?

She didn't have much experience with men; she'd been awkward in school, and then soon afterward she'd gotten attached to Hank. She wasn't the flirtatious, frequent-dating type. So she couldn't tell what vibe Danny was putting out. Did he want to date her? Couldn't he read her lack of interest in him?

As she got out her notes and ordered coffee, she cast a glance in the direction where Buck had roared off and frowned. Why had he put this insecurity into her head? Why couldn't he accept that women could be businesspeople, meeting with other businesspeople? That it wasn't always about dating?

"We're really looking forward to working with you," Danny said after their coffee had arrived. "Have you thought any more about what your business might entail? Had the chance to look at any storefronts?"

"Not really, Danny. I've been totally occupied with getting Lacey's house ready for the festival."

"How's that going?" he asked, and she told him about what they were doing. "That's great, great," he said. "But let's focus on your business as soon as that's over."

She frowned. "Can I ask why you're so interested in working with me? I'm not a high-capital investor, believe me."

"Oh, we like to help small-business people in Rescue River. It's a community outreach kind of thing. Keeping the downtown strong."

She nodded, studying him without making it obvious. He just didn't seem sincere. "I have to give all of it some thought."

She wished Buck were here so she could ask him his opinion, learn more about Danny's background. If only he weren't so touchy about her having coffee with another man! With concern, she realized that Buck was the person she most trusted right now, most wanted to share the details of her life with, big and small.

When did *that* happen?

"You're staying in town, though, right? You'll be here through the festival and beyond?" He looked so eager that, against her better judgment, she was flattered. Even though she wasn't going to pursue a relationship with him, it was nice to have a man show interest.

"I'm planning to stay, at least for a while,"

she said. "Rescue River is a wonderful place. So warm and safe and welcoming."

An odd expression flashed across his face and then was gone. "Right," he said smoothly. "Rescue River *is* a safe place."

And as they parted ways, she wondered again why Danny was so interested in her business, even though she'd been open about the fact that she didn't know how long she'd be able to stay.

That afternoon, Buck drove Gina out to pick up Bobby in a thoughtful mood. As he waited for them in the truck and then headed back to Rescue River, he considered his own progress.

In the past, he would have been royally mad that Gina had had coffee with Danny against his advice, to the point where he couldn't have had a reasonable discussion. He remembered, with some embarrassment, a couple of occasions when he'd gotten jealous about Ivana. Both had led to huge fights.

But today, he'd managed his feelings with just a little mild argument.

And out by the Rescue River sign last week, when Dion had flashed his lights, he hadn't freaked out. Yeah, he'd been startled, but he hadn't grabbed Gina and taken her to the ground or some crazy move like that.

Counseling and AA and prayer must be starting to have an impact, even on a hard-headed creature like him.

Gina cleared her throat like she'd been trying to get his attention for a while. "Hey," she said. "If this is too much trouble, I can start asking Angelica to bring me home."

"What?" He glanced over at her and was surprised to see her lower lip out and her eyes blazing. "It's no trouble. What are you talking about?"

"You've been completely silent during this whole drive. You didn't even say hi to Bobby!"

"Well, excuse *me*." Was he supposed to put on some kind of show for her? He paused, took a breath. *She's a woman. She has different needs.* "I'm sorry. I didn't know I was acting weird."

"You're not sulking about my having coffee with Danny Walker?"

He frowned, thinking. "I'm not thrilled about it. I don't trust the guy."

"So you *are* mad." There was the satisfaction of being right in her voice.

"No." He shook his head. "You're an adult. And…although I feel a lot for you, we're not a couple. I don't have the right."

They were driving through Rescue River now, getting close to the guesthouse, and he didn't want to leave things like this. On an impulse, he pulled over beside the town park. "Look, since I neglected Bobby before, how about we take him to the playground for a little bit?"

He turned off the truck and looked at her. There were two vertical wrinkles between her eyebrows, and her lips pressed together.

"We don't have to," he said. He put his

hand back on the keys, waiting for the put-down that might be coming. You never knew with women.

But then she smiled, her cheeks going a little pink. "Okay. Sure. That would be great."

Happiness flooded him. He'd been able to get her from upset to happy. He *was* learning, maybe at a slow pace, but still. He came around to her side of the truck, opened the door for her and helped her out.

Her hand was soft, delicate. He pulled in a breath.

She shot a glance at him and then got very busy unhooking Bobby from his car seat in the back.

He shouldered the diaper bag while she carried Bobby, wiggling with excitement, on her hip.

"I have to say," she said as they headed toward the play area, "I *was* uncomfortable with Danny this morning."

"What did he do? Did he make a move on you? Do you want me to talk to him?"

"No, no!" She laughed a little. "I just... Well, I question his motives."

"I can tell you his motives," Buck groused.

Her laugh rang out like a bell. "I love this park," she said, waving her hand around. "We didn't have this kind of friendly-feeling place in my neighborhood in California."

"I used to play sports here as a kid," he said, accepting the change of subject. "And do less wholesome things when I was in high school."

"You're such a bad boy." She rolled her eyes and then looked wistful. "This must have been a great town to grow up in."

"It was." And for a second, Buck got a hard, hot yearning to stay, to raise a family here like had been the plan with Ivana and Mia.

They reached the playground, and Buck set the diaper bag down on a bench. A couple of moms on the other side of the colorful play structures stood talking while their kids climbed the taller one, yelling out their after-school joy. Off in the distance, someone was stringing lights and people were unloading something from a truck, probably getting ready for the festival at the end of the week.

Gina carried Bobby over to a bucket-style swing and eased him into it, and then stood in front while Buck pushed it gently from behind, making Bobby giggle each time he swung toward his mom. A light breeze rattled the still-bare tree limbs and the sun warmed the back of Buck's shoulders.

When Bobby tired of the swing, Buck lifted him out and helped him toddle over to a play structure. Bobby pulled himself up and climbed through an opening, landed on his hands and then pulled himself through. Immediately, he turned around and did the same thing again.

"He is *so* close to walking." Gina squatted down and reached into her pocket, then looked at the basic flip phone with disappointment. "Oh, man, I wish I'd brought my other phone to take a picture!"

So Buck pulled out his phone and snapped a bunch of photos and a video—of Bobby, mostly, but also of his pretty mom. She'd be happy to have memories of herself and Bobby together as he grew.

He sure was a cute kid. As cute as Mia had been, though in a different way. Sadness and nostalgia washed over him, but gently, a spring shower rather than a storm.

He could think about Mia now. And yeah, it hurt, a lot. That was only natural. Losing her and Ivana would always be the biggest sadness of his life.

He glanced up at the sky, pale blue with fluffy white clouds scudding by. Mia and Ivana were with Jesus now. And he didn't know what heaven was like, but he was sure that mother and daughter were together and happy. Maybe there was a big swing set somewhere up there.

His throat tightened. He swallowed, then focused on Bobby. "Come on, little man. Ever gone down a slide before?"

* * *

Gina watched as Buck lifted Bobby halfway up the plastic slide, then whooshed him down. As Bobby laughed, Gina's heart melted a little.

Buck was so kind. Even when they were arguing, even when she'd been a teeny bit unreasonable, he didn't blow up or sulk. Instead, he tried to make things right.

She was starting to trust that Buck had her best interests at heart, that he wasn't trying to manipulate her the way Hank—and, yes, her father as well—used to do.

Moving to the bottom of the slide, she knelt down so Bobby could glide into her arms, safely guided by Buck. A couple more trips, and he wanted to wander over to a low play table. She helped him, and he stood banging the table like a drum.

"Sit down over there," Buck said, pointing to a smooth stretch of rubberized play surface. Then he lifted Bobby and set him down a few yards away, holding him by his shoulders. "Walk to Mommy," he said.

Gina's mouth dropped open. "Do you think he can?"

"Call him," Buck said. "I won't let him fall."

So she held out her arms to her son. "Come on, sweetie."

Bobby chortled and lifted one awkward leg after the other, staggering unsteadily toward her. Buck was supporting him—and then he wasn't.

Never taking his laughing eyes off her, Bobby toddled into her arms.

"Oh my word! His first step!" She was laughing and crying at once as she pulled Bobby to her and hugged him tightly. Such joy. And such sharp pain that Hank wasn't here to see it.

A movie of memories flashed through her mind, the good ones this time: Hank in the delivery room, flourishing the scissors as he fearlessly cut the cord. The way he'd insisted on taking Bobby to visit every friend he had, the moment the pediatrician had okayed it, just to show off his brand-new son. How he'd swept her into a huge hug when they'd seen Bobby's first smile.

Hank hadn't been perfect, not by a long shot, but he had loved his son. And he would have loved to see this milestone.

Buck knelt beside her and wrapped both her and Bobby in his arms.

Tears flowed down Gina's face even as she laughed and kissed Bobby. "I'm happy and sad at the same time," she said to Buck.

"Me, too." His voice was a little choked.

She looked into his eyes and realized it was true. He'd lost as much as she had. More.

She tightened her arms around both of them—Buck, who'd seen so much, and Bobby, who was only beginning to explore the world. Closed her eyes and lifted a wordless prayer.

Bobby struggled free, used Buck's arm to pull up to a standing position and then looked from her to Buck expectantly. "Go!" he demanded.

"Has he said words before?" Buck asked, laughing as he scooted a few yards away and held out his arms for Bobby.

"Not that clearly." Gina wiped her eyes and steadied her baby and let him go, lurching from leg to leg with undeniable independence.

The next day after his lunchtime AA meeting, Buck stopped by the hardware store as planned. He picked up a few needed supplies while he waited for Mr. Love to finish giving detailed instructions to his granddaughter, who'd run the store alone in his absence.

"I got this, Granddad," she said good-naturedly. "You can take an hour off to do some visiting!"

Reluctantly, Mr. Love headed out the door. Buck crooked his arm for the older man and alerted him to curbs during the three-block walk to the Senior Towers.

"Now, see," Mr. Love said, lifting his face to the spring sunshine, "isn't this nicer than riding in a car? Not that I didn't appreciate the offer. But any chance to be active and outside, I take it."

"A good philosophy." Buck listened to the birds singing in the trees, just beginning to offer a few buds, and smelled the earthy scent of spring. He'd like to share in that feeling of new life, but truthfully, his insides were in turmoil.

He'd spent more time with Gina and Bobby during the past week than during any of the previous weeks since she'd arrived in town. They'd worked long hours, and tag teamed on child care and cooking and dog walking, since Crater and Spike were now established residents of the guesthouse. They'd shared conversations about their pasts, argued amiably over final paint colors and finish details, and generally made a great team.

They'd shared Bobby's first step.

Passing the Chatterbox Café made him

think of Gina meeting Danny. He shouldn't begrudge her starting to establish other friendships, and he didn't—as long as the friendships were female. But Danny Walker's obvious interest in Gina bothered him.

Danny was too slick for Gina, and he didn't think them a good match, but then again, he had no right to comment on or criticize her choices. What say did he have?

"What's got you bent out of shape?" Mr. Love asked.

"Who says I'm bent out of shape?"

"It's more than obvious. You're wound up tighter than a drum. And I'm a fast walker, but you're rushing me here. Cut me a break. I'm eighty-seven!"

"Oh, man, sorry!" He slowed down. "And… you're right—I'm a little uptight."

"Woman problems?" Mr. Love asked.

"Now, why would you jump to that conclusion?"

Mr. Love chuckled. "I couldn't help noticing the attention you paid to that young lady in the hardware store. Gina? Is she going to be there today?"

"She'll be there." Buck debated denying everything, but Mr. Love had known him a long time. "And yeah," he said. "I like her. But she's got issues, especially with addicts and drunks. And I'm leaving town. *And* someone else is after her."

"You've got problems." Mr. Love nodded. "Serious problems, but there's one thing— you're not defined by being a drunk. Kid I knew, who worked so hard in the store, he wasn't a drunk."

"I've changed."

"Yes, you have. More than once. A man can be forgiven for going a little crazy after the losses you had, but that doesn't mean you'll be crazy forever. You seem kinda sane to me right now."

"Maybe."

"And why are you leaving town? Rescue River is your home!"

Buck shook his head. "Burned too many bridges. Bad reputation. I need to start fresh."

"Like my mama used to say, no matter where you go, there you are. You think your problems won't follow you into another town?"

Buck guided the man around a broken section of sidewalk. "That's exactly what I think. In another town, they won't look at me like the criminal who busted up a restaurant or got his license taken away."

"You're going to give up your woman just so you don't have to have hurt feelings?"

The question echoed in the air, and Buck wondered: Was that what he was doing? "Sounds kind of cowardly," he admitted.

"Yes, it does. And you've never struck me as a coward."

Buck blew out a breath. "Speaking of women...anything you want me to do to promote your case with Miss Minnie Falcon?"

"Hey, hey now." Mr. Love held up a hand. "Show respect for your elders."

Buck chuckled. "You can dish it out…"

Mr. Love bumped a fist into Buck's upper arm. "We almost there? I'm getting tired of talking with you."

"As a matter of fact, we are. But I've got my eye on you." Buck was grinning, satisfied with having turned the tables on the old man.

When they walked into the homey, plant-filled lobby of the Senior Towers, Gina and Miss Minnie Falcon—and a whole cadre of Miss Minnie's friends—were waiting for them.

"Trust a man to be late," Miss Minnie said, leaning forward to check the grandfather clock. "No sense of time."

Buck took a breath, but Mr. Love squeezed his arm, communicating nonverbally not to respond.

"They're right on time," Gina soothed, "or maybe a few minutes late is all. Should we head up to your apartment, Miss Minnie?"

"We should. I've got everything all ready."

After a few words with the other women

in the lobby, the four of them went upstairs and were soon looking through the trunk of materials Miss Minnie had saved or inherited over the years.

"We're looking for something from 1850 or thereabouts," Gina said, her face flushed with excitement. "How much do you know about what's in here, Miss Minnie?"

"I surely do wish I could see better," Mr. Love said wistfully.

"There are letters from some of my ancestors," Miss Minnie said. "And drawings, jewelry, even some early photographs. A good deal of family history."

"We'll respect your privacy," Gina said. "Are you sure it's okay with you if we go through it?"

Buck loved that about her, that she was sensitive to the older woman's concerns. Gina hadn't had an easy life, and maybe that was how God was using her trials: to make her kinder than the norm.

"It's perfectly fine. I'm so old now, I don't care who knows my business."

"I know exactly what you mean, Minnie," Mr. Love said.

Miss Minnie blushed. "Look for a pair of daguerreotypes in a brown leather case. From what you've told me, they'll be very interesting to you."

Buck and Gina knelt in front of the trunk and opened the lid. Inside was a jumble of letters, a blue military uniform, jewelry in worn velvet cases and pewter candleholders.

Gina sat back on her heels, very close to Buck. "Wow, Miss Minnie, this is awesome! It belongs in the historical society for sure!"

"If we had one, I'd gladly donate it to them."

Buck carefully picked up a brown leather case. "Is this the one?"

"I believe," Miss Minnie said, "that those photographs are images of the couple in your old diary, Abraham and Minerva."

Gina's eyes sparkled as she studied the images: on one side, a beautiful African American woman in an elegant wedding dress; on the other side, a handsome white man in a formal suit, including a vest and short tie. "So they did get married!" She practically glowed with excitement.

Miss Minnie shook her head. "No, dear. Those photographs were taken weeks before the wedding was to happen. You'll notice the style of dress conceals her pregnancy."

"I imagine any pictures had to be taken in secret, given the times and her status as a runaway," Mr. Love said.

"Wait—I'm confused." Buck was studying the photograph. "Did she have Abraham's child?"

Miss Minnie shook her head. "It wasn't Abraham's child, you see. She arrived pregnant. She'd been assaulted by a plantation owner down South."

"How awful," Gina breathed, glancing over at Buck.

"I respect the fact that he was willing to

marry her in that circumstance," Mr. Love said. "It must have been quite unusual back then."

Miss Minnie nodded. "What happened to her was awful, and yet if she hadn't found a safe place to bear her baby, I wouldn't be here."

"You're a descendant?" Buck looked up from the trunk. He'd known Miss Minnie for years, ever since she'd been his Sunday-school teacher, but he hadn't known that she had a slave ancestor.

"That's right. Miss Minerva Cobbs was my great-grandmother."

"Wow. You were named after her," Gina said.

"Yes, young lady, and proud to be. Since that day, there has always been a Minerva in the Falcon family."

Buck was impatient to hear the end of the story. "You said they didn't marry. Did she decide to move on with the others headed north?" Buck was remembering his Ohio history. "Because the Fugitive Slave Act would've put them at risk, right?"

"The rest of the group wanted her to come with them. They were worried Abraham would take advantage of her, that he wasn't serious about marriage, but they were wrong."

Gina moved a little closer, her shoulder brushing Buck's, and he felt his blood pressure rise. Did she know what she was doing to him? He leaned back against the couch and put up a pillow for her back, and she scooted back and sat right next to him, the side of her leg burning into his.

He shot up a prayer for calmness.

"Tell us what became of them," Gina asked, seemingly unaffected by their closeness.

Miss Minnie shook her head, looking sad. "Like many women of those times, she died in childbirth. But Abraham and his parents raised her son, Ishmael, as their own and gave him their last name."

Mr. Love whistled. "Even despite his mixed race."

"They were staunch abolitionists and strong Christians. They believed all people were equal."

"Wow." Buck tore his attention from the woman beside him to focus on the story. "There are people nowadays who could learn a lesson from your ancestors."

"They very nearly made a full-time job of assisting fugitives to freedom. It's said that eight hundred people came through the Falcon home." Miss Minnie smiled proudly.

"That's amazing!" Gina was practically rubbing her hands together. "We have *got* to tell this story."

"Miss Minnie should be the judge of that," said Mr. Love. "She may not want it known that she has some mixed blood."

She inclined her head at him. "My father was one of Ishmael's five sons, the youngest, and he inherited the house. And while he didn't advertise his ancestry, he didn't hide it within the family, nor in Rescue River. He always encouraged me to be proud of my great-grandmother, and I am."

"And you should be." Gina gripped the older woman's hands. "But what do you think about making it public? There's no pressure to do that."

"It's not widely known," Miss Minnie admitted. "In fact..." She trailed off and looked at the floor as if lost in thought.

"Are you okay, Miss Minnie?"

"I've never married," the older woman said. "But I was engaged. When my fiancé discovered my background, he broke off the engagement."

"For racial reasons?" Gina asked. "That's awful."

She nodded. "I'd left this area, gone away to school. People in other places weren't as open as those in Rescue River."

Mr. Love shook his head. "My, my. I always wondered why a fine-looking woman like you didn't have a husband. You had plenty of suitors as a schoolgirl."

Miss Minnie chuckled. "I did make a few conquests, didn't I?"

"Hearts were broken, right and left."

Buck didn't ask, but he wondered whether Mr. Love's heart had been one of those broken, or at least bruised, by a younger Miss Minnie.

"And so you stayed single," Gina said.

"Don't feel sorry for me, young lady. I've had a wonderful life in this town. And it may be that I don't have the temperament for marriage. I always did have strong opinions of my own, and when I was young, not many men could tolerate having a wife on an equal plane."

"Not many men in your circle had any sense," Mr. Love said. "Why, I would have…" He shook his head. "But times were different then."

"Yes, they were."

As the two elders began sharing stories of people they'd both known in years past, Buck glanced at Gina to find her watching them, her face a study in care and concern. As if in common accord, they moved to the trunk and started sorting through the items now brought to life by the story they told.

Ribbons and photographs and letters. "Where do we begin to sort these out?" he asked quietly.

"We start small," she said. "I think we should find just enough to make a display for the Freedom Festival. And if Miss Minnie is feeling up to it, maybe we could ask her to come talk to visitors."

"Mr. Love as well," Buck suggested. "He's done presentations for the festival before." He looked up to ask Mr. Love about it, but he was talking intently to Miss Minnie, their heads close together.

He turned back to Gina and found her lifting an eyebrow at him. "Senior romance?" she whispered.

"Love is beautiful at any age," he said, and Mr. Love's example gave him courage to reach out and touch Gina's shoulder, gaze into her eyes. "We may have barriers, Gina, but it's nothing like people faced in times past."

She looked from the old diary in her hand to him and then back again, color rising to her face.

He touched her chin. "No pressure," he said, "but maybe, when things settle down, you'll give this a little thought."

She looked at him, her eyes darkening. "Give *what* a little thought?" she almost whispered.

He let his hand caress her soft cheek and tangle in her hair. "Us," he said. "Give *us* some thought."

That night, Buck was going into the Star Market just as Dion was coming out.

"Any news about the mysterious buried treasure?" Dion asked, grinning.

Buck filled him in on the conversation they'd had with Mr. Love and Miss Minnie.

Dion whistled. "I had no idea. Definitely

need to record them telling their stories, and sooner rather than later. Did she know anything about the ring you were hunting for?"

"You know, in the midst of all the story-telling, we completely forgot to ask."

"Makes sense."

Buck was about to turn away when he thought to ask Dion about Gina's California in-laws. "Hey, any news about Gina's situation?" He knew Dion had been monitoring the police airwaves and had also contacted colleagues in California to keep updated.

Dion lifted his hands, palms up. "It's strange," he said. "According to my friend in California, there was a ton of inquiry and investigation for the past couple of weeks. But yesterday, it stopped."

"Stopped?" Buck tilted his head to one side. "What do you make of that?"

Dion shrugged. "Maybe they've given up."

"Maybe," Buck said.

"Or maybe... I don't know. Let's keep our eyes open."

"Will do," Buck said, an uneasy prickle crawling up his neck.

Two days later, Gina finished the dishes, strolled toward the sitting room and looked in. Buck was there, leaning back in a big chair with Bobby on his lap, turning the pages of a board book. In front of the fireplace, Crater and Spike nestled on a folded blanket, and Mr. and Mrs. Whiskers curled up together on the back of the couch. Pretty lamps stood on end tables, and paintings of local landscapes graced the walls. They'd all worked late last night, dragging furniture out of storage, to get several of the rooms finished.

She stopped in the doorway to survey the scene, her heart swelling with happiness.

Her son was thriving here, that was the main thing. He got all the attention he needed, and even though he had a case of the sniffles, Buck was cuddling him close. He treated the boy like kin.

She took pride in the beautiful room. The walls were a light chocolate shade, set off by white moldings, and this afternoon they'd put up the ornate chandelier she'd found in a local antiques shop. Heavy gold draperies added weight and warmth, and the chesterfield sofa and wing-back chairs gave the room the look of an old library.

At that moment, Buck looked up and saw her, and the light in his eyes sent warmth all the way to her toes. Maybe they had a chance after all.

"Ready?" he asked. They were planning to do the finish work on the final room tonight, in preparation for the start of the festival tomorrow.

"I'm ready. But you two look comfortable."

"We are. He's a little stuffy." Buck studied Bobby and brushed his wispy hair off his forehead. "Almost asleep. Can he stay down here with us?"

Touched by the big veteran's care for her son, she scanned the room. "We'll be right next door. He can rest in here." She folded a couple of blankets, put them on the floor and set up the baby monitor.

They worked in the connected room as the sun slanted low and golden, making hazy squares on the polished wooden floor. Gina painted baseboards with glossy white enamel while Buck put a door back on its hinges.

Buck set his phone to play quiet contemporary music. They chatted a little as they worked.

Gina's heart was full to breaking. After tomorrow, this interlude of renovation would be done. Lacey could find someone else to do the work, or she and Buck could do it themselves at a more leisurely pace.

And whether Gina stayed in Rescue River or moved on, her time of working closely with Buck would likely come to an end.

She didn't want it to; she wanted to go on working with this man. Her attachment to him was growing daily, and her fears about his past were lessening. She was starting to think that maybe, just maybe, she'd fallen for a winner this time.

But he wouldn't be around. He had a plan and knew what he needed. And that was, apparently, to leave Rescue River.

She finished her painting and tapped the lid back on the can, then stood to survey the room.

"Penny for your thoughts," he said, coming up behind her.

She looked over her shoulder at him. "This has been fun, renovating the place," she said, surveying the room. "I'll miss it."

"You're talking like it's over."

"You know what Lacey said. Only until the festival—no more."

"Okay," he said, "but you'll stay in Rescue River. Right?"

"I don't know. I'd like to stay, hire out as a historical renovation consultant or open a shop for interior decorating, but I'm not sure it would be wise to take that on." She sighed. "It's a lot of responsibility, being a single parent, you know?"

She felt him nod behind her. And then he put his arms around her and pulled her back against him. "Whatever happens," he said, "I hope you know you've got a friend."

But, oh, she wanted more. "Is that what we are? Friends?"

"What do you think?" he asked, his breath warm against her ear.

The feel of his arms enfolding her, warming her, circling her, set her heart pounding. She felt him nuzzle her hair. The music swelled and the light was dying and the poignant contentment made her close her eyes. "I think I could stay like this forever," she whispered.

His arms tightened, and for a moment, they just breathed together, their whole bodies in sync.

Suddenly, the dogs went crazy, Spike's hysterical yip combining with Crater's deep growl.

And then, before she could step away from Buck to investigate, she heard a sound and saw a sight she'd hoped never to experience again: her former mother-in-law, holding Bobby, standing in the connecting doorway. "How nice," Lorna said. "You're cozying up to a derelict while our grandson rolls around on the floor with the dogs."

Chapter Twelve

Buck took in the situation instantly.

"Art! Lorna!" Gina's voice was a breathy gasp. Based on her stricken expression and the well-coiffed older couple's words, these had to be Gina's husband's parents.

The sight of that fist-size bruise that had marred Bobby's leg when he first arrived came back to Buck. Bobby's grandparents. His *abusive* grandparents.

Two long steps put him directly in front of them. "Bobby needs to go to his mother. Now."

He reached for the baby.

The older woman turned away. "Step back,

young man," she said, her voice scornful, but also a little scared. "Don't you dare touch me or this baby."

"I don't want to touch you," he said, "but if you don't give Bobby back to his mother right now, I will."

He'd commanded men to do things they'd never have risked on their own. He'd frightened macho Afghan militants into backing down. Dead drunk, he'd glared down punks with guns in the seediest parts of Cleveland.

Never had his powers of intimidation felt so important.

Gina seemed to draw from his strength; she came and stood beside him and held out her arms.

The older woman looked sulky, but then some kind of nonverbal signal passed between her and her husband.

She handed the baby to Gina.

Gina seized Bobby, pulled him close against her shoulder and stepped back. Her face was white. "How did you find us? What are you doing here?" She ran her hands over Bobby's arms and legs as if she was worried that they'd already hurt him.

The man, Art, stepped between Buck and his wife and turned his back, effectively excluding Buck from the conversation. He was probably six feet tall, his sports jacket stretched across his shoulders, his khaki-clad legs planted wide. He crossed meaty arms over his chest and glared at Gina. "Did you think we couldn't find you, with our connections?"

She swallowed visibly and clutched Bobby closer. "You don't have connections in Ohio," she said in a hoarse voice.

The woman cackled. "We know people everywhere. We aren't like you, a nobody from nowhere."

Buck mentally scanned through everyone he knew in Rescue River, wondering who would run in these folks' elevated social circles. Sam Hinton, maybe? But Sam would swallow glass before he'd betray a woman and child in need.

"Our friends Bernice and Jerry Walker just happened to see their son's post about a new guesthouse on social media," the woman said. "They thought the woman and baby looked familiar. They got in touch with us, and we spoke with their son."

Gina gasped. "Danny Walker. And those publicity pictures Amy was taking that one day. I never even thought—"

"After he met with Gina and assessed the situation for us, he was concerned," Art interrupted. "He saw you getting involved with someone you shouldn't. Said that you and Bobby were practically homeless."

Betrayal was written all over Gina's face.

"And I must say," Lorna added, looking around the room, "he was right to be concerned. You're working as a common laborer."

"Place is dirty." Art brushed imaginary dust off his sleeve.

302   *The Soldier and the Single Mom*

"And our grandson, lying on the floor unsupervised, with a couple of dirty, dangerous dogs. He could have been bitten."

"Or hurt on these nails and wood." The burly man nudged at a small pile of scraps with his toe.

"Art. Lorna. Come on. There's a baby monitor, and the dogs are perfectly safe," Gina said. But her voice sounded insecure.

Buck felt a quake of doubt, too. *He* was the one who'd suggested that Bobby stay downstairs with them.

But he'd trust Crater with any child, and Spike wouldn't hurt a flea.

Whereas these folks had already hurt Bobby. "You're trespassing in my sister's house," he said. "Get out."

"Door was unlocked," the man, Art, said. "Anyone could have walked in. You might want to think about that."

"It's a safe town," Gina said. "Or was, until the two of you came in."

Dion. Buck needed to call Dion.

He got out his phone and scrolled through his contacts, tapped Dion's name. "You need to get over to the guesthouse," he said the moment Dion answered, not trying to hide his words from either Gina or Bobby's grandparents. "The people who abused him before are here. Gina needs help."

"Be right there," Dion said.

Lorna's penciled-on eyebrows lifted almost to her hairline. "*We're* the danger? Us?"

The man pointed at Buck, thumb and forefinger out like a gun. "We know all about you, son. If anyone's a danger to Bobby, it's you."

"We talked to the nice people next door, in the Senior Towers," Lorna said, hands on hips. "They told us about *your* reputation. Drunk all over town, breaking places up, getting yourself arrested. Why, the very idea of our grandson anywhere near you has us terrified."

"And not that she's treated us well," Art

said, "but we'd hate to see Gina take up with the likes of you."

"Do you even have a job, aside from day work?"

"We heard you're in AA but that you were also seen at a bar recently."

"Once an alcoholic, always an alcoholic."

Gina was looking at him, her eyes stricken. "You were at a bar recently?"

"Not to drink," he tried to explain. "Not to drink."

But the words, true as they were, sounded false in his own ears. Like the excuses he used to make to Lacey. Like the lies every alcoholic knew exactly how to tell.

"You're a danger to both Gina and Bobby," Lorna declared. "We'll certainly take steps to keep you away from our grandson. And, Gina, what on earth were you thinking, leaving safety and comfort in California for this?" She swung a scornful arm around. "For *him*?"

The words went on, spoken by all three, an

argument the older couple was clearly winning. It all started to blur together in Buck's head as he backed slowly out of the room and toward the guesthouse's front door.

What *had* he been thinking, getting so close to a nice woman and her innocent baby? Thinking he could have a normal relationship with them, be good for them, even?

He'd been the downfall of Ivana and Mia, and he was headed toward being the downfall of Gina and Bobby.

He opened the door and stepped onto the front porch. He had to get out of here. Had to make Gina and Bobby safe by leaving. But he couldn't go until she had another protector.

"If you think you'll be able to keep custody after this, you're wrong," he heard Art say through the screen door.

"When we go back to California, we're taking Bobby with us," Lorna added.

A police car squealed to a halt in front of the house, and Dion was out of it and up the porch stairs in seconds. When he saw Buck, he stopped. "Fill me in."

"The grandparents from California. Making threats, scaring Gina and Bobby." As if to back up his words, a loud wail came from inside the house.

Dion nodded and hurried inside, leaving the door open like he expected Buck to follow. When Buck didn't, he looked back, eyebrows lifted. "Come on, man."

But Buck knew what was best for everyone, and he wasn't it. He grabbed his wallet and keys. "You handle it," he said and headed out, bent on getting far, far away from here.

Gina survived the next hour of shouting and accusations by clinging to Bobby, soothing him, reminding herself to stay strong for him. She reeled from the force of Art and Lorna's hatred, her stomach churning with fear. Could they take Bobby from her?

Could she prevent them, with her complete lack of money and power?

Her mind darted in all directions, but it kept coming back to one question. Where was Buck? Why wasn't he here, standing by her?

Of course, it wasn't his problem or his obligation. She shouldn't feel betrayed. Still, she'd trusted him and felt he was a friend, if not more.

If not a whole lot more, if their sweet embrace was any indication.

But now, in her hour of need, he seemed to be gone. True, he'd gotten Dion here, for which Gina was incredibly thankful, but still. She'd expected something different from him.

Then again, if he'd been frequenting bars...

As Art and Lorna talked heatedly to Dion, heaping on accusations and innuendos, Gina shot up prayers for help and safety with every breath, her body cringing from the onslaught of lies and bitterness that seemed almost physical in its intensity. She didn't see how God could deliver her, but she tried desperately to remember all the biblical promises she'd ever memorized.

Dion was a force of calm and reason. Obviously sensing that she was near her breaking point, he pulled Art and Lorna aside for quiet moments of conversation while she took Bobby upstairs to calm down. As she let him nurse, she prayed hard, and bits of verses came back to her.

The Lord is my strength and my shield.

We are more than conquerors.

Thou preparest a table before me in the presence of my enemies...of my enemies...of my enemies.

She wanted to stay in her room, to shut out the hateful forces downstairs. But she needed to pay attention. She couldn't shrink away as she used to do.

She put Bobby down in his crib, but he fussed and lifted his arms, so she picked him back up and carried him downstairs, stopping in the doorway of the living room to listen to what was going on.

"You wouldn't understand," Lorna was saying in a patronizing voice. "You people are used to all that drinking and rough behavior."

Gina blinked. Had Lorna really said that? To *Dion*?

"Did you want to elaborate on just what kind of *people* you mean?"

Lorna hemmed and hawed.

"I didn't think so." His answer was quiet, with steel underneath. "Now, I suggest you go back to where you came from and leave the decent folks of Rescue River alone."

Art and Lorna both started talking at once, even as they backed toward the door. Phrases like *back tomorrow* and *with a warrant* and *custody hearing* and *abducted out of state* flew from their mouths.

Gina stepped out of the kitchen in time to see Dion take a couple of steps toward the couple.

They turned and left, slamming the door.

Gina sank down onto a bench in the entryway. "I'm so sorry about them," she said to Dion. "They're awful."

"I can see that." He leaned against the wall, looking through the window beside the door as a car engine started up outside. "But it's not your fault."

The sound of spitting gravel as the car sped away took some of the weight off Gina's heart. "I caused them to come here and disturb your town."

He shook his head. "That was their decision. We just have to make sure they don't get access to Bobby."

"You knew about his bruises?"

He nodded. "Your in-laws aren't the only ones who have connections. Did you ever get a restraining order against them?"

"I tried. The officer I talked to advised against it." She paused. "They donate a lot to the local police fund-raisers."

Dion just shook his head.

Car headlights flashed through the window, and fear clawed at Gina's stomach. Had Art and Lorna come back?

Or had Buck? Now, after the trouble was temporarily over? She braced herself to yell at him, but truthfully, all she wanted was the protection and comfort of his arms.

But it wasn't Buck who came through the door. It was Lacey.

"Hey, guys, are we all set for tomorrow? I heard we're supposed to have record turnout at the festival…" She broke off, seeing Dion. "What's wrong? Where's my brother? What's he done now?"

Gina flinched. Lacey, who knew him so well, had made the automatic assumption that Buck had gotten into trouble.

The truth clicked into place, like pieces from a puzzle. His sister assumed he'd fallen off the wagon. He'd been seen at the bars.

She blew out a breath as her hopes and dreams about him shattered around her. She'd thought he was a great guy, wonderful. She'd even begun to dream of a future together.

But he is *a great guy!*

Yes, he was. Her husband had been, too, when he wasn't high.

But she knew where this road led. Despite the twists and turns, despite the promises and the calm periods, and, yes, the happiness, in the end, what you got was a couple of cops on your doorstep.

Ma'am, are you Gina Patterson? We have some bad news...

Her eyes filled with tears as disappointment congealed into a huge lump in her stomach. When would she ever learn? Why had she let it happen again? She had to understand that love wasn't meant for someone like her, too needy, too hopeful, too ready to look past fatal flaws when they came in the guise of a charming guy, someone like her dad.

She couldn't subject Bobby to that. But look at her—earlier tonight, she'd been ready to jump into Buck's arms, to make a commitment that she and Bobby would be his family.

She was a fool.

Dion and Lacey were talking quietly, glancing over at her. She heard Buck's name. And then they both took their phones out, punching in numbers. Waiting.

No answers.

Gina felt the same discouraged hurt that was written on Lacey's face, the same tight-lipped anger that flattened Dion's mouth.

Buck hadn't cared enough about her and Bobby to stay. The siren call of the bottle had been louder to him than Bobby's cries.

She knew it was an illness, that he couldn't help himself.

But he was helping himself! He was in recovery! You never saw him drunk, not even once!

But if he was well and whole, he'd be here now.

They all waited for another hour, drinking coffee, checking phones, talking a little. Gina took Bobby upstairs and put him to bed, then came back down. Too restless to sit, she cleaned up the little bit of remaining mess in the room she and Buck had been working on.

Before everything had gone straight downhill.

When she came out, Dion was shrugging into his jacket. "I've got to get back on patrol, but I'll make sure you're all locked down," he said. "We'll have frequent surveillance. And, Lacey, you stay here with Gina and Bobby, okay?"

Gina opened her mouth to protest, then closed it again. She didn't want to be an obligation. But Bobby's safety took precedence over her own embarrassment.

"Of course." Lacey moved to stand by Gina. "We'll be fine."

After Dion checked the locks and all the downstairs windows, he drove off with another promise of frequent patrols.

Gina turned to face Lacey. "I'm sorry to have involved you in all this. I know you didn't want us here, and that you've been working extra to avoid being around us, getting all your memories kicked up. As soon as I can find a way to keep Bobby safe, I'll be out of here and you can go back to life as normal."

Lacey took her hand and tugged her into the kitchen. She filled the kettle with water and put it on the stove. And then she came to sit across the table from Gina. "It may not seem like it," she said, "but you and Bobby have been a help for me. Forced me to face some things about myself. To get my thoughts and plans together." Lacey closed her eyes for a minute and then opened them again. "It's been painful. But I understand some things better now. I'm not going to *get* better, not completely."

"Oh, Lacey, with God's help—"

"I know." Lacey held up a hand. "I'm praying all the time, looking for guidance, asking for forgiveness. And I realize I'm never…" She swallowed hard.

The teakettle whistled, and she stood and

poured hot water over tea bags, brought two cups over to the table.

"We don't have to talk about this now," Gina said. "It's late. I'm sure you want to go to bed."

"Do *you* want to? This has to have been an awful, scary day. I don't know the whole story, but you must be exhausted."

"I'll never get to sleep. If you can distract me by talking about something other than my horrible in-laws, go for it. Please."

Lacey dunked her tea bag repeatedly, not looking at Gina. After a moment, she spoke in a low voice. "I realize I'll never be able to love a man and child again. Not like I loved Gerry, problems and all. And maybe that's why..." She broke off, opened her eyes wide as if that would make the tears stay inside. "That's why God made me infertile. Why I can't have another baby."

"Oh, Lacey." Compassion for the other woman flooded Gina's heart, making her own worries recede. "Are you sure?"

"Pretty sure. I just got results from a few more tests."

"And here I've been preoccupied with work and all my problems and never even thought of what you might be going through. I'm sorry. That must be so hard to deal with."

Lacey grabbed a napkin and started shredding it. "It's like I'm frozen inside. Maybe I'm going to stay that way. But when I get over this initial…hurt, I'll figure out what to do with my life as a single person. There's nothing wrong with being single."

Gina nodded. She needed to start remembering those ideas herself. "That's what the Bible says."

"Exactly. And maybe that's His mercy to me, stopping me from even trying to connect with a man and have a family. Because I can't." Her voice was quiet and bleak.

"Oh, Lacey, don't give up if that's your dream. There's all kind of medical advances, there's adoption, there's—"

"I know," Lacey interrupted. "I know, and

I know it's not going to happen for me. But let's get off my issues. I feel like a rat, talking about this when your baby's at risk."

"I *want* to talk—"

"No." Lacey raised her hand like a stop sign. "Please. I can't… Look. I've got a burglar alarm, and Dion made me turn it on. The locks are great—Buck made sure of that. We'll be safe through the night. And things will look better in the morning." She blew out a breath and banged the table with a fist. "I just can't believe that brother of mine. I thought he was making such good progress."

"Me, too." Gina's voice broke a little and she pressed her lips together.

They finished their tea in silence and then hugged good-night and went upstairs.

"Tomorrow is another day," Lacey said.

Gina nodded. *Another day when Bobby's at risk of being taken from me.*

Chapter Thirteen

Buck didn't know how long he drove. It could have been minutes, or it could have been hours. Finally, when he couldn't outrun his pain, he pulled off the highway into a little rural strip mall's parking lot.

It looked familiar, and he figured he'd been here before. In his drinking days, he'd spent a fair amount of time traveling, doing odd jobs, letting whatever town he was staying in cool off.

There was a Chinese restaurant at one end of the strip mall, still open, and he thought about going in to get tea and something to eat. But since the place looked familiar, had he been here before? In what condition? He couldn't face another manager barring the door, another rejection.

The words of Gina's former in-laws rang in his ears.

Drunk all over town.

Once an alcoholic, always an alcoholic.

A danger to Bobby and Gina.

It was that last one that hurt his heart and scared the daylights out of him. Bobby and Gina meant the world to him. He loved them both—he knew that now. He wanted them to be his family.

Only, if he was a danger to them, then no dice. He couldn't put them at risk. If he were the cause of someone else dying, another woman and child…well, that would be unforgivable. Better to keep running and never come back than to harm them in any way.

He remembered his wife's words in their final bad days. *Terrible husband…don't know why I married you…disaster as a father.* He'd had enough counseling to know that words spoken in anger couldn't fully define who he was. At the same time, if the sources all agreed, then you'd come upon truth.

Even the people at the Senior Towers had condemned him. His old friends, the people who'd known him since childhood.

And Dion…his disappointed expression when he'd looked back and seen that Buck wasn't coming along. It was a killer.

The truck cab was getting stuffy, and he needed to move. He got out and leaned back against the side of the truck, looking around the small plaza. Yes, he'd been here before, had seen that dollar store, that gas station.

He knew without looking behind him that there was a bar across the street. His back actually tingled, as if the place were pulling him magnetically toward it.

He was far enough from Rescue River that no one was likely to know him there. He had money. He could easily go in and get a drink or a couple. No one from home would find out.

And even if they did, who cared? His reputation was already in the sewer.

Some part of his mind recognized the dangerous direction of these thoughts, and he fumbled in his pocket for his sobriety coin. But he was still wearing work clothes, and he hadn't put the coin in his pocket this morning. Had missed doing it a lot of days lately, in fact. He hadn't been thinking about alcohol.

He'd been thinking about Gina.

He blew out a breath and tried to latch on to what he'd learned in AA. He should call his sponsor. He reached back into the car, and only then did he realize he didn't have his phone on him. He'd left in such a hurry that all he'd grabbed was his wallet. His phone was on his dresser at home, turned off so it wouldn't wake the baby.

Bobby.

He looked heavenward. "I've tried, Lord. I've really tried here."

Of course, there was no answer. God wasn't

on speaking terms with a loser like him. God was in agreement with all the good people of Rescue River.

He banged a fist against the top of the car, stupidly. It hurt, and he winced as he climbed back in and started the engine.

Washing his mind clean of any thought, he drove over to the little bar's parking lot, pulled up close, got out.

As he approached the door of the road-house, a light flashed next door. Curious, he looked over.

It looked like another bar beside the first one, only where the first bar flashed beer signs, this one had the message—Jesus Saves—along with a blinking cross.

He hadn't seen it the last time he was here. Lacey would have called it tacky.

Was it some kind of joke? But no, above the door was a small sign: New Country Church. Along the storefront windows were painted slogans and verses: "Sinners Saved by Grace" and "All Welcome" and "Because He Loves You."

Buck shook his head. Some crazy Christian, or a bunch of them, making a church along the highway. Trying to, anyway. He had to admire the effort, however futile. How would a church compete with a roadhouse full of light and color, with pulsing music, laughing people?

Whereas the little church…

Ridiculing himself for being a fool, he walked over to the door. A Thursday night, late—no way would it be open.

He tried the door.

It opened.

"Really, God?" he said out loud. Took one last glance back at the roadhouse. Then walked into the storefront church.

The next morning, Gina was already up and dressed after a restless night, feeding Bobby, when there was a pounding at the door.

Lacey didn't come down, and Gina wasn't

sure whether or not she'd left for work. So she answered the door herself, Bobby on her hip.

Standing on the porch was Dion in full uniform, and Daisy, a woman Gina had met briefly at the church lunch.

But Daisy acted official rather than friendly as she shook Gina's hand. "Daisy Hinton. I'm a social worker, here to look into a couple of things for Children and Youth. Is this your son?"

Gina's heart pounded so fast she thought she might pass out. "Yes, this is Bobby," she said and clutched him tighter.

"May I come in?"

"Okay." Gina stepped aside.

"I'll leave you to it, then," Dion said to Daisy. "Call me if you need anything. I won't be far away."

In the hall, Daisy took off her coat. "We had a report of child neglect. I'm just here to ask a few questions."

Gina's knees went limp and she sank down

on the hallway bench, clutching Bobby so tightly that he fussed a little. They'd done it. They'd reported her. She was going to lose her son.

He leaned his head against her and clutched her hair in stubby fingers, and she straightened her spine. No way would she let them win.

"You can't take him." Gina stood and gauged the distance to her car, wondering whether she could outrun this woman. No doubt Dion's presence and assurance that he was near was meant to forestall just that.

"No, that's not what this is about. Not at this point. Can we sit down and talk?"

Manners. Show her you're a good mom. Gina gestured the other woman into the kitchen. "I'm sorry—I'm a little upset. Would you like some coffee?" She looked at the high chair where Bobby had eaten his breakfast. Cereal was scattered over the tray and on the floor, and there was a smear of banana on the chair itself. Too late, she noticed that some of it was in his hair as well.

Why, oh, why hadn't she cleaned things up before answering the door?

"No coffee, thanks. Can you tell me a little about your routines with Bobby, where he stays while you're working, that sort of thing?" As she spoke, Daisy watched Bobby, not staring, just observant.

Gina blew out a breath and tried to speak, but no words came. She reached for her own coffee and lifted it, thinking it would calm her, but her hand shook so badly that she sloshed some out onto the table and banged it back down too hard.

"Hey," Daisy said gently, "it's okay. Take a minute."

The kind tone brought tears to Gina's eyes. Still, she knew she shouldn't trust it. Daisy was just trying to get her to open up.

Never had she felt so alone. Sure, she liked it here in Rescue River; she'd made a start at some friendships. But the reality was that she was new in town, not really a part of things. She was an outsider, and it was her word against two other outsiders, Bobby's grandparents, so much more wealthy and powerful than she was.

The one real friend she'd thought she had was notably missing: Buck. He hadn't come in last night, as far as she knew; he must be out carousing or else sleeping it off. She'd chosen the wrong person to attach herself to, as usual.

The loss of him, of who she'd thought he was, opened up a hole in her chest, so painful she almost gasped with it.

Bobby struggled to get down and she set him on the floor, then immediately wondered if that was the right thing to do. Lacey kept the kitchen clean, but the mat below the high chair held the remains of breakfast.

Daisy watched as Bobby pulled up on the chair and moved toward his race-car push toy. A couple of steps, and he fell forward onto his hands, then moved into his preferred crawling mode. Gina went over to make sure he didn't run into anything, and Daisy stood, too.

"Seems like his development is normal," she said. "What's he doing lately?"

That, she could talk about. "He's pulling up a lot and taking a few steps, like you just saw. He's not steady yet." Remembering how he'd taken his first step when Buck was watching, her throat tightened. She'd felt so close to Buck then. She'd trusted him.

Bobby pushed his car into the hallway and down, banging it into the doorway of the front room. He looked back at Gina. "Da? Da?"

"He wants the dogs," she explained, and then her hand flew to her mouth. "Is that bad, that I let him be around the dogs? They're gentle as lambs, but my former in-laws were upset..." She trailed off, not wanting to incriminate herself.

"Being around animals is actually good for babies. Helps them not get allergies."

"That's what I've read." Relieved, Gina opened the door and Spike and Crater cried to get out of the crates they stayed in at night.

She opened the crates, picked up Bobby and let the dogs go outside. "Sorry," she said over her shoulder. "Mornings, they need to get out and get fed."

"I understand. I'm Troy Hinton's sister, after all. I know rescue dogs, and I know Crater." She gave the large dog a head scratch as he bounded back inside. His tail wagging, Crater soaked up the attention and then ambled toward the kitchen, pausing to lick Bobby a couple of times. Bobby giggled and sat down hard on his diaper-clad behind.

Gina's adrenaline spiked again. Was that bad, letting a dog lick a baby? But it was too late to change it.

Spike tore in, barking, and ran in front of Crater to get to the kitchen. "He thinks he's the alpha," Gina explained. "And Crater lets him think so. Do you mind if I get them their breakfast? They'll settle down after that."

"I have all morning," Daisy said, "and this is actually great, to see your household, and your care of Bobby, in action."

Way to make me self-conscious, Gina thought as she scooped dog food into bowls. But the daily routine relaxed her a little, as did Daisy's apparent friendliness.

Don't get too trusting, she reminded herself.

"So," Daisy asked, "while you're working on the house, where does Bobby stay?"

Gina tensed. "Sometimes we—I mean, I—I gate him in an adjoining room. Sometimes he's in his jumper, although he doesn't like it as much as he liked his jumper in California. He doesn't like to be confined." She looked down at Bobby, only to realize he was crawling rapidly out of the room. "Bobby!" She put down the dog food and hurried over to close the kitchen door. "Exhibit A," she said and pulled out a couple of pots and pans for him to bang.

"Do you have alternative care if you're

doing something he shouldn't be around?" Daisy asked, so Gina explained about Angelica.

They walked around the house slowly, with Gina showing Daisy the places Bobby played, his toys, his crib. As they talked about his routines, Gina started to relax. Daisy just didn't seem like an enemy; she seemed fair.

After they'd gotten back to the kitchen, Daisy sat down at the table and pulled out her tablet computer. "I'm going to make a few notes here, if you don't mind," she said. "No guarantees, but I don't see anything that would warrant removing Bobby from the home."

Relief washed over Gina, and she offered a quick prayer of thanks.

Daisy typed rapidly on her tablet, and Gina started wiping down the high chair while Bobby pulled more pans out of the cupboards.

The kitchen door opened. "Hey," Lacey

said. "I slept in a little, since I'm off today. Daisy, what's up?"

"Just looking into a few things." Daisy tapped away on her tablet.

"Like, professionally?"

Daisy nodded, still typing.

"The in-laws," Gina explained. "They filed a report against me and she's investigating."

"What?" Lacey stared. "You're the best mother I've ever seen!"

Gina's jaw just about dropped. "I... I have to say I'm surprised, but thanks."

Bobby had picked up a plastic bowl, and now he put it on his head, making them all laugh. Gina hurried to get it off so he wouldn't be scared, but they were still laughing when Art and Lorna flung open the kitchen door. Spike barked fiercely from behind Gina's legs while Crater walked out to stand, alert, in front of the intruders.

"Where's our grandson?" Art demanded.

"I don't recall inviting you into my home," Lacey said.

"We were given to understand a social worker would investigate. Can't you quiet down that dog?"

"I'm a social worker, and I'm investigating," Daisy said calmly, snapping shut the case of her tablet. "Come here, Spike. Good boy." She swept the little dog up onto her lap.

"But…but it looks like you all know each other," Lorna argued. "That's hardly a fair investigation."

"In this town, we all know each other," Lacey said.

"And we like it that way," Daisy added.

Gina swung Bobby to her hip and stepped forward, empowered by the other two women's presence. "And that's why I want to raise Bobby here," she said. "It's a warm, safe environment. A real community. He'll grow up happy here."

Lorna's hands went to her hips. "Once we get a *real* investigator in here, I'm confident that our home will be determined to be a better environment for him."

Gina's stomach dropped. Could they do that? She wouldn't have thought so, but she'd been surprised before at what their money could buy.

She opened her mouth to protest, but Lacey stepped forward and put an arm around Gina. "Since you're uninvited guests and this is my home, I'd like to ask you to leave."

Crater stepped forward with them, emitting a low, almost inaudible growl.

Lorna took a step back, but Art huffed and didn't move.

"I have the police on speed dial," Daisy said pleasantly. "Shall I call them?"

"Come on, Lorna. Once I make a few phone calls, they'll be singing a different tune." The older couple turned and walked out onto the front porch, and Gina followed to make sure they really left.

And there was Buck, trotting up the steps, looking much the worse for wear.

"You again!" Lorna sputtered. "So it's true you live here. We ought to have you arrested. A common drunk in the same house as our grandson!"

Dion's police car cruised slowly by, and Art hurried toward the street to flag him down.

"He's not…" Gina broke off. She didn't know *what* Buck was or wasn't. She couldn't deny the burst of happiness in her chest when she saw him, but she couldn't trust it, either.

"What are *you* still doing here?" He asked the question of Lorna, politely, but with steel in his voice.

"Getting ready to take custody of our grandson, if it's any of your business."

"No, you're not." Gina lifted her chin and glared her in-laws down. "I'm through putting up with your manipulation and…and abuse. Bobby's staying here with me, and that's that."

"Abuse? You've been watching too many trashy TV shows."

"I saw Art hit him." She narrowed her eyes at Lorna. "And you were holding Bobby still so he could do it. Don't even try to deny it."

"I do deny it," her mother-in-law said, her lip curling. "And no one's going to believe you over me."

"I think they will. Wait here. Everyone, please." Buck pushed past Lorna and into the house, giving Bobby a brief chin tickle that made him chortle, looking into Gina's eyes with something inexplicable in his own. Then he disappeared up the stairs.

Hearing some noise on the street, Gina stepped out onto the porch. Dion was walking toward the house with Art, but something off to the side made him stop and stare.

Gina looked, and then she stared, too.

From the direction of the Senior Towers came a parade of white-haired people, some striding, some using walkers and some being pushed in wheelchairs.

They appeared to be headed…here.

When they reached the gate in the front of the guesthouse, the clatter of canes and the scrape of wheels on concrete trailed off. The crowd parted to allow Miss Minnie Falcon to march to the front, her eyes blazing.

Instinctively, Gina went down to meet the older woman, holding Bobby on her hip. "What's going on, Miss Minnie?"

"I'll tell you what's going on." She stopped her walker and drew herself up, pointing a long, bony finger at Art, then at Lorna. "We were having breakfast this morning when word came around that you two are attempting to take little Bobby away from his mother."

"And that they're using things we said as evidence, which is just plain ridiculous," Gramps Camden contributed from the front of the crowd.

Behind Gina, the door of the guesthouse opened. She looked back as Buck hurried out, still in his bedraggled clothes, and then stopped. Crater stood at his side.

"For one thing, that young man," Miss Minnie said, gesturing at Buck, "is a fine, upright person, and any child would be safe with him."

Gina blinked at the vote of confidence.

Ninetysomething Bob Eakin, the Towers librarian, came forward, adjusting his Proud WWII Veteran baseball cap. "He may have had some troubles in the past, but who here hasn't?" he asked, his voice ringing out loudly. "Who will cast the first stone?"

Realization swept over Gina. She *had* been casting stones, had been believing the worst of Buck even against the evidence of her own senses. "Buck Armstrong is totally safe," she said. "I'd trust him with Bobby's life."

Buck descended the steps slowly, his forehead wrinkled. He opened his mouth as if to speak and then closed it again.

"And what's more," said Lou Ann Miller, who was pushing a wheelchair, "Gina Patterson is a wonderful mother. I've visited her and seen her with Bobby. There's no reason on earth to take that baby away."

Seeing the white heads nodding, Gina's

throat tightened. When in her life had people ever stood up for her this way, taken her side?

Art made an abrupt, waving gesture, seeming to discount their words. "The truth will come out, and then we'll get custody."

Buck took an intimidating step forward, and despite his ragged clothes, his straight posture and steely gaze made everyone quiet down.

"The truth *will* come out. I had occasion to take a picture of Bobby right after he and his mother arrived in Rescue River," he said, holding up his smartphone. "And if you'll look where I'm zooming it in, you'll see the fist-size bruise on Bobby's leg." He looked at Gina. "I'm sorry to make your story public, but these people have to be stopped. The reason she left California," he said as he turned to the crowd, "is that these two were beginning to abuse their grandson. This bruise is just the outward mark of some pretty awful behavior."

Art and Lorna sputtered and looked at each other. Before they could formulate a response, Dion's voice boomed out. "Is that true, Gina?"

She cleared her throat so she could say it loud and clear. "They hit him and shook him. I was afraid for his safety."

A murmur came from the Senior Towers crowd, rising in volume. Indignant voices stood out.

"That's an outrage."

"They should be prosecuted."

"We don't tolerate that kind of thing around here."

Lorna's face was red and her eyes shiny with tears. Art looked apoplectic. "You haven't heard the end of this," he snarled at Gina. "It's not against the law to discipline a child."

Dion stepped toward the couple. "I'll be following up with my colleagues in California. Now, I'd suggest you get out of our town and don't come back."

Assenting voices came from the white-haired crowd.

Art and Lorna looked at each other, then turned and hurried down to their car, hunching away from the disapproving stares and comments of those watching. A moment later, their car pulled away.

Gina stood, dazed, as voices and activity swirled around her. Finally, a gentle hand patted her back. "I brought down a chair," Lacey said. "Come on—sit."

So she sank into an Adirondack chair, Bobby in her arms, and Lacey sat down beside her. Spike jumped up, licked her leg and Bobby's, and then squeezed in beside her, panting. And as people came up to express their indignation or sympathy, offering help and comfort, something long empty inside her started to fill. She was cared for. She was protected. She was home.

Chapter Fourteen

It was now or never.

Buck hitched his duffel to his shoulder and walked out into the moonlight. He'd thought about it all day today, had prayed, had found moments between the busy festival activities to discuss things with Lacey.

He'd gotten his life and his sobriety back in Rescue River, had learned he could love again. He'd even, at the storefront church, come to see that he wasn't to blame for Ivana's driving off the road with Mia. But he was still some distance from being fully recovered, and he didn't know if he'd ever get there. The wise pastor he'd talked to last night had reminded him of what the Bible said about being single: it could be a blessed state, allowing a person to devote himself to God's work.

But Buck knew he couldn't get to that point while being in Gina's presence. He'd come to care too much. At the same time, he'd seen how she didn't trust him, might never trust him, because of her own past. The minute Art and Lorna had started lobbing accusations, she'd believed them.

He didn't blame her for that; he did have a past, and so did she. But he owed it to himself and to God to go somewhere he could make a difference and rebuild a life.

He'd debated over and over whether to talk to her before he left, but in the end, he'd decided that a quick departure would be less painful for both of them. He'd left a letter for her with Lacey, explaining why he was leaving.

He strode out the front door, intent on reaching his truck before he changed his mind.

"Where are you headed?"

The soft voice nearly shattered him. Slowly, he turned toward the source of it: Gina, on the front porch, bathed in moonlight and holding Bobby.

Nod and run! His brain made that very practical suggestion. But his heart and soul tugged him toward the pair, so he dropped his duffel by the rocking chair and walked over.

Gina smiled at him, looking relaxed. She'd always been gorgeous, but from the time she'd arrived in town, tension had tightened her face and haunted her eyes. Now that was gone, and the effect of her genuine, full smile was stunning.

"Wh-what are you doing out here?" he stammered, buying time.

"I finally got him to sleep." She nodded down at Bobby, relaxed in her lap. "But then he woke up again, all fussy. Sometimes fresh air and rocking helps him settle down."

"And you can relax now, knowing you're safe here," he said.

"Exactly. I never felt quite at ease bringing him outside at night. Silly, I know, but I worried that Lorna and Art would jump out and grab him."

"I don't think they'll be bothering you anymore." He believed it, too. He'd followed them when they left downtown with their tails between their legs, had watched them check out of the motel at the edge of town and made sure they drove away. He'd spoken to Dion this afternoon, and the full force of the law had been in effect. Dion was in contact with the police in the couple's hometown and was working on a restraining order here. If a trial came, Gina would have to testify, but after his conversation with Lorna and Art, Dion was certain they'd stay away.

"Thanks for what you did with the picture," she said. "In the confusion afterward, I couldn't find you. I wanted to make sure to tell you, I think that's what turned the tide."

"Only after you spoke up and told the truth." He shrugged. "And Miss Minnie did a pretty good job of telling them off."

"She did, for sure. But it wasn't until the whole town—and Dion—saw that picture that we really got rid of them."

He looked up at the stars, breathed in the smell of night blossoms. Now that he was here with Gina, he might as well talk a little. Besides, it would take a while for his brain to regain control and make him leave. "I should have stayed with you when they first came. I had something to work out, but I shouldn't have left you."

"I was upset you did," she admitted. "Pretty mad at you, in fact, but it all turned out all right." She put a hand on his arm. "You're not perfect, Buck, but you're a good man."

Just like that, he was forgiven. He shifted and knocked a boot against his duffel and it tipped out into the middle of the porch floor. She looked at it, then at him. "You're leaving?"

He looked down at the duffel, then up at her. "Yeah."

"Again, without telling me?" There was hurt in her voice.

"I wrote you a letter. Lacey has it." He looked out across the silvery, quiet street. Should he go into it with her? Would he be able to leave at all if he stayed here, talking with Gina in the moonlight?

Talking with the woman he loved?

The answer, obviously, was no.

He forced himself to stand up. To put his duffel over his shoulder. One step at a time.

Bobby stirred, then opened his eyes and saw Buck. "Buh! Buh!" he said sleepily, holding up his arms.

Buck picked the baby up, a lump in his throat. This inimitable little man had helped him to heal, and Buck hated to leave him. "Hey, it'll be okay," he said, jostling the sleepy boy.

Don't go, then, his heart mourned. *Stay!* "I could..." He started. Then stopped himself.

No. Don't reopen that door. "See you," he croaked out, handing Bobby back down to Gina. And then he turned and walked slowly down the porch steps, feeling older than any resident of the Senior Towers.

Gina watched him go with a perfect storm of pain and confusion swirling inside her.

Why was he leaving? Because he *didn't* care for her, or because he did?

Because he was honorable or dishonorable?

"Buh," Bobby fussed, reaching toward the vacant spot where Buck had been.

Babies and dogs, they could sense who was a good person. And she could sense it, too. She hadn't trusted herself, and she hadn't made good decisions in the past, but she'd changed. Grown. Toughened up.

If Buck were a danger to her and Bobby, she'd let him go, no question. But she knew with every fiber of her being that he wasn't a danger, that he was, in fact, perfect. Not a perfect, flawless person, maybe—there weren't any of those—but perfect for her.

The sound of his truck starting pierced the darkness, and suddenly she was on her feet, clutching Bobby to her hip. She rushed down the steps to catch him. "Buck! Wait!"

But he was already pulling out in the street, his jaw square, face grim. He didn't look to the right or left, but only forward. And he drove away.

Despair gripped her heart. If he left, would he ever come back? Would he know she cared for him? That she loved him?

She walked out into the street, looking after him. She was wearing flannels and a T-shirt, fuzzy slippers on her feet, a robe billowing around her in the slight breeze. She looked like a fool.

Moonlight illuminated the shops, now dark and empty of people. The streetlamps cast a soft glow. She loved this town. But it wouldn't be home without Buck.

She started speed walking down the middle

of the street, Bobby tight against her chest. She passed the Senior Towers, where one or two windows still glowed, and thought of the parade of helpers that had come to save Bobby today.

She wanted to stay here, to raise Bobby here. But she didn't want to do it alone.

"Buck! Come back! Come back!" She started running down the middle of the main street of Rescue River, the robe flying behind her like wings, chasing those two red taillights. Waving her free arm frantically. "Hey! Come back!"

The lights were getting dimmer. She slowed to a walk, straining her eyes.

She couldn't see the taillights. He was gone. She blew out a sigh that ended in a sob and stood, holding Bobby in the middle of the downtown she loved.

"Come back," she whispered. "Please, come back."

But there was no sound except the rhythmic croaking of a couple of frogs in the creek. No sign of a truck turning around or coming back.

Bobby's fussing rose to a wail, and she felt like wailing, too. She couldn't—she had responsibilities—but she felt like it.

Despair made her shoulders hunch over as she carried her crying son back toward the guesthouse.

He had to do this. He couldn't look back.

He put on his turn signal, being careful even though there was no other traffic on the road. By the book, by rote—that was the only way he could force himself to leave Gina and Bobby behind.

He started to turn and glanced in his rearview mirror. He thought he saw something back in the middle of the downtown.

What was that? Billowy, floating, but half looking like a woman?

Memories slammed into him, of that first night he'd encountered Gina and Bobby on that lonesome road outside town. So much had happened since then. He'd relearned how to feel, how to love. He'd grown to where he could put aside his own past, his temptations, because that was best for the people he cared about. The two people he cared about most in the whole world.

The truck was coasting into the turn and he couldn't help it; he stopped and looked back, squinting through the darkness.

There was definitely someone there.

He'd better go back just to make sure it wasn't someone intent on harming Gina and Bobby. Some lowlife sent by her rich former in-laws to scare or threaten them.

He turned the truck around and headed back, slowly, trying to see.

Clouds skittered over the moon, throwing the street into darkness. He let the truck coast quietly, watching.

And then his heart gave a great thud. It was Gina, walking back, head down.

Walking slowly, as if she'd come out into the middle of the street.

As if she'd been chasing him.

If there were any chance at all…

He pulled the truck crookedly into a diagonal parking place and got out, not even bothering to close the door. "Gina! Wait!"

She turned. Her eyes widened. "Buck?"

"What are you doing out here?" He strode toward her. "I… I just had the thought…" He hesitated. And then realized he needed to put his pride aside and tell the whole truth. "Gina, if you have any interest in pursuing this thing we've got…"

Her free hand went to her mouth, her other arm around Bobby. Slowly, her eyes never leaving his, she nodded her head.

He was in front of them in two seconds, wrapping his arms around her right in the middle of Main Street. "Gina, I promise you, I've changed. I'm a new man, with a new life."

Her eyes got shiny, and as she stared up at him, a tear spilled out.

He reached down and thumbed the dampness from beneath her eye. "I know you've got baggage, and the Lord knows I do, too. But with God's help…"

That gorgeous smile spread across her face, and it was like the sun coming up. "With God's help, we just might make it work."

"You're willing to try?" He was laughing a little and yet his own throat felt tight. "Gina, I love you so much you wouldn't think there was any extra room in my heart, but there is, because I love Bobby just about as much as I love you."

She stepped into his embrace. "I love you, too," she murmured against his chest.

"Buh," Bobby said sleepily. "Buh. Buh."

They both laughed a little and cried a little. "Come on," he said, wrapping an arm around her shoulders. "Let's go home."

Headlights flashed behind them. Buck shepherded Gina and Bobby to the sidewalk.

A marked car pulled up beside them—Dion. "Everything okay here?"

"More than okay," they both said at the same time. Then laughed.

Dion gave them an assessing look. "You left your truck running, buddy, but I'll take care of it. Looks like you've got something better to do."

As they walked back to the guesthouse, Gina clutched his arm, making him stop. "But what about your reputation, the troubles you've had here?"

"I still have some reparations to make," he said, "but this community is forgiving. I figured that out yesterday, when the seniors all defended me." He smiled down at her. "When *you* defended me."

"We take care of each other here," she said.

"And you? You're okay being with someone who'll probably go to AA meetings for the rest of his life?"

"Absolutely," she said, moving closer to his side. "I trust that you've turned a corner."

He had turned a corner, Buck reflected as they climbed the stairs together. And he was sure glad he *hadn't* turned the corner out of Rescue River. Because this was the start of the new life he'd always wanted.

Chapter Fifteen

The last day of the festival was drawing to an end when Gina came downstairs, having just gotten Bobby up from his nap. She carried him toward the front room, pausing to stand in the doorway.

Buck was there, and Gina's breath caught when he smiled at her. They'd spent almost every moment together since Friday night, talking and dreaming.

It was as if the Lord had taken away all her anxiety and stress, and she was able to accept that Buck loved her, that she was lovable and that this was God sanctioned and could work. Feeling his arm around her as they'd walked through town yesterday, taking in the festival, had been bliss.

At the front of the room, Mr. Love and Miss Minnie Falcon sat telling the story of their ancestors and how the house had served as one of the most prominent stations on the Underground Railroad. They'd held visitors rapt both days, and they were thriving on the questions and interest.

Bobby started babbling, so Gina backed away, not wanting to detract from the elders' storytelling. Lacey waved her over to the front desk. "Look at this," she said, showing Gina the computer screen.

"What am I looking at?" Gina leaned closer. "Are those…bookings?"

Lacey nodded, beaming. "Starting this fall, we're booked every weekend up until Christmas." She blew out a breath. "Which means we'll have to work like crazy to get this place done, but with all these reservations, I'm feeling confident enough to cut down to part-time at work so I can help, too."

"That's wonderful!" Impulsively, Gina hugged the woman.

"I owe it to you," Lacey said. "You believed in what could happen before I did, and your work and PR abilities are what tilted the balance."

Gina leaned back on her elbows, looking around. "It does look great. And what's happening in there—" she gestured toward the front room "—that's just serendipity. Good for everyone."

"It's good for me, seeing you and Buck together," Lacey said. "He deserves happiness." She looked wistfully into the room, where her brother was kneeling to help Mr. Love hold up the large door, with its tiny peephole, that had camouflaged the fugitives' hiding place in the basement of the Falcon home.

"Your time will come."

Lacey laughed. "I wouldn't go that far. I'm just glad to see my brother happy. And you. And those two crazy rescue dogs."

"Things are going to get even crazier when my California dogs come home. My friend Haley is driving them when she comes to visit next month." But it would work out. She had faith that everything would work out, now.

As the last group of guests filed out of the front room, Gina slipped inside. Mr. Love waved to the last visitors, and then he leaned over and said something to Miss Minnie.

"Why, Mr. Love," Miss Minnie said, her cheeks pink. "I hardly think that's appropriate at our age."

"I've buried two wives, and I'm not looking for another," he said calmly. "But there's nothing wrong with companionship. And a man is never too old to appreciate a beautiful woman." He patted Miss Minnie's hand.

"Except I know you can't half see," she complained, but a smile lit up her deeply lined face.

Mr. Love turned to Buck and Gina. "Miss Minnie and I, we've been talking, and she helped me look through some of the heirlooms we had out at the old farm. I found something pretty special, as this young man knows."

Gina looked at Buck and was alarmed to notice perspiration on his upper lip and a pale cast to his face.

"I've had an offer for this particular item," Mr. Love continued, "that I'm tempted to accept, but only if the buyer can put it to good use." He pulled out an old velvet box, just a couple of inches square. "The young couple who were going to use this more than one hundred and fifty years ago never got their happy ending. This has been in a cubbyhole in the Old Rose Barn ever since, waiting for the right time to be found."

"We can't help them," Miss Minnie said, "but maybe we can help to create some happiness right here and now."

"I'm hoping." Buck took the box from Mr. Love and walked over to Gina, drawing her toward the high-backed love seat. "Sit down a minute."

Gina's heart rate kicked up a notch, and she did as he asked.

The two elders watched, smiling, obviously in on some secret. Lacey was leaning on the doorjamb, smiling as well.

Buck knelt in front of her. "Gina," he said, "you know how I feel about you, and I want to ask you, will you marry me?"

"What?" Her voice rose to a squeal.

He opened the box, and there was a Victorian-style gold ring, its central diamond surrounded by small diamonds that formed the shape of a cross.

Gina's breath caught. "Minerva and Abraham's ring?"

Buck nodded. "You haven't answered my question." His hands shook a little, holding the ring box.

Joy rang through her like bells. "Of course! Yes, yes, yes!" She tugged him to the seat beside her.

"There's only one condition," Mr. Love said, "on my selling Buck that ring."

"What is it?" Gina asked.

"Anything," Buck said at the same time, so fervently that he drew a laugh from Lacey, still standing in the doorway.

"That the person wearing it has to stay right here in Rescue River." Mr. Love flashed a smile. "We don't want you going anywhere."

"Why would anyone want to live anywhere else?" Miss Minnie glanced over at Mr. Love, and a dimple appeared in her cheek.

Tears sprang to Gina's eyes. "I'll stay," she said, and then she couldn't get out any more words. She just nestled closer to her future husband's side.

The sound of barking came from the next room, where Spike and Crater had been confined to their crates, safely out of the way of the festival's guests. Lacey disappeared, then returned a minute later with the dogs bounding in beside her, in hot pursuit of Mr. Whiskers. Mrs. Whiskers, who'd been weaving through Buck's and Gina's feet, jumped up on one arm of the love seat, and Mr. Whiskers leaped onto the other arm. Both glared indignantly down at the raucous canines.

Buck chuckled, then touched Gina's chin, turning her face toward him for a kiss. And, safe in his arms, Gina knew that she and Bobby had found the home and family she'd always craved.

* * * * *

If you enjoyed this book, pick up these
other RESCUE RIVER stories
from Lee Tobin McClain!

ENGAGED TO THE SINGLE MOM
HIS SECRET CHILD
SMALL-TOWN NANNY

Available now from Love Inspired!

Find more great reads at
www.LoveInspired.com

Dear Reader,

I hope you've enjoyed this latest trip to Rescue River, Ohio—a fictional town that incorporates some of my favorite things about my home state. For this book, I dug into the history of the Underground Railroad in Ohio. I also researched renovation and decor of historical houses…and veterinary tools…and twelve-step programs. I love all the things I get to learn about as I write my books. Yes, I'm a nerd!

Buck Armstrong first appeared in Rescue River as a minor character with a drinking problem, back in *Engaged to the Single Mom*. At that point, I certainly didn't envision him as a hero with his own romantic story. But as people keep telling Buck, and as he finally comes to believe, people change…with God's help. When he can embrace the fact that he's a new creation, he can be the husband Gina deserves and the father little Bobby needs.

If you would like to keep up with all of my

news and book releases, stop on by my website, http://www.leetobinmcclain.com. Sign up for my newsletter, and you'll get a free story as a gift. And please come visit Rescue River again to read about Buck's sister, Lacey, whose story comes out later this year.

Blessings,
Lee